A Summer on Thirteenth Street

A Summer on Thirteenth Street

○ ○ ○

Charlotte Herman

DUTTON CHILDREN'S BOOKS   NEW YORK

The author gratefully acknowledges permission to quote, on
pages 51 and 52, from "Praise the Lord and Pass the Ammunition"
by Frank Loesser. Copyright © 1942 by Famous Music Corporation,
copyright © renewed 1969 by Famous Music Corporation.

Library of Congress Cataloging-in-Publication Data

Herman, Charlotte.
    A summer on Thirteenth Street / by Charlotte Herman—1st ed.
       p.   cm.
    Summary: World War II affects Shirley Frances Cohen, her
buddy Morton, Manny—who joins the army—their parents, a
German immigrant suspected of being a spy, and the other people
in their Chicago neighborhood.
    ISBN 0-525-44642-7
    [1. World War, 1939–1945—United States—Fiction.   2. Chicago
(Ill.)–Fiction.]   I. Title.
PZ7.H4313Su   1991   91-21156
[Fic]—dc20   CIP
                                                           AC

Published in the United States by Dutton Children's Books,
a division of Penguin Books USA Inc.
375 Hudson Street, New York, New York 10014

Printed in U.S.A.   First Edition
10   9   8   7   6   5   4   3   2   1

To the Barans
of Thirteenth Street
and the
Great West Side (GVS)

· *1* ·

Shirley Frances Cohen stood on the corner of Thirteenth Street and Independence Boulevard, watching the two sailors who were walking toward her. There were always lots of sailors on the boulevard these days. They were all over Chicago, in fact. Shirley knew there was a naval base nearby, where the sailors took their training before going off to fight the war against Germany and Japan.

"Go ahead, I dare you," said Morton Kaminsky, who was peeling the bark off a branch with his pocketknife.

"I'll do it when I'm ready," said Shirley. She bent down to tie the laces on her brown oxfords and then straightened up and tucked her polo shirt back into her slacks.

"I'm ready," she announced, glancing at the approaching sailors. Shirley thought they were the cutest things, in their white hats and bell-bottoms. If only she were a boy, she would be a sailor someday and get to wear one of those snappy uniforms.

When the sailors were just a few feet away, Shirley ran up alongside of them, and in her best Betty Grable style, said, "Hi there, sailors. How about a date?" She winked.

It was hard for Shirley to be Betty Grable. Betty Grable was a blonde with shapely legs, and Shirley was a brunette with long braids and skinny legs. Her mother thought she was beautiful, like that other movie star, Hedy Lamarr. She winked again.

The sailors didn't even stop. But they smiled, and one winked back. "Some other time, gorgeous."

Shirley giggled. She didn't really expect a date with any sailor. And besides, she wasn't exactly sure what a date was or what she would do with one if she had it. She ran back to Morton.

"Did you hear that?" she said, and then she lowered her voice in imitation of the sailor. " 'Some other time, gorgeous.' " She giggled again.

"I'm going to be a Marine," said Morton. "They're the toughest of them all." He threw away the branch and stuck his knife back into his pocket.

Morton was short and round, and it was kind of hard for Shirley to picture him as a Marine. He looked nothing at all like the Marines on the posters that hung in stores all around the neighborhood. The ones that said WANT ACTION? JOIN THE U.S. MARINE CORPS. She decided that he was more the pilot type because of the leather cap and pilot goggles he sometimes liked to wear.

"I've got a cousin who's a Marine," Shirley said. Actually, her cousin was just a third cousin, but Shirley left that part out.

They headed down Independence toward Douglas Boulevard to Zelnick's Drugstore. Shirley and Morton each had a quarter for a malted. It would be their first malted of the summer. It was also their first day of summer vacation. School had let out early that morning, and Shirley and Morton had been the envy of their fifth-grade class when they were asked to stay behind and help Miss Mulhern clean up. They got to clean out her drawers and closet, and wash the blackboard, and take home a lot of great junk like construction paper, old workbooks, ink eradicator, and a relief map of Albania.

Now they had a whole summer ahead of them. And for Shirley, there was no season quite like summer. Summer was beautiful, and it seemed to last forever.

"Race you to Zelnick's," Shirley said without warning. And she was off and running.

"Hey, no fair," Morton shouted from behind. "You had a head start."

Running and laughing at the same time, Shirley shouted back to him, "It doesn't matter. You still can't beat me." She sucked in a mouthful of air and burst ahead, letting the air out in small puffs, trying to keep up with the Chicago Motor Coach bus that sped alongside her on the boulevard. She ran faster and faster. Faster than a speeding bullet, more powerful than a locomotive. She was a bird! She was a plane! She was Super-Shirley!

She landed in front of the drugstore and turned around just as Morton caught up to her.

"You cheated," he said, breathing hard.

"I did not. Besides, even if I started a second before you, I came in at least three seconds ahead."

"Three seconds, my eye," said Morton.

The door to the drugstore was open, and while Morton made his way to the soda fountain, Shirley stopped by the candy counter. Maybe, just maybe, today would be the day. She squeezed her eyes shut and made a wish. "Please . . . just one small piece."

"Whatcha standing here for?" asked Morton, coming back to get her.

Shirley opened her eyes and searched the counter. Nothing—as usual. She let out a long, tired sigh. "I was hoping there would be some bubble gum today," she said.

"Don't waste your time looking," Morton told her. "There won't be any until the war's over."

Shirley knew that Morton was right. The bubble gum shortage, along with sugar and coffee rationing, was one of the many hardships of war. It was awful. You just couldn't get a piece of Fleer Dubble Bubble anyplace. The gum was being sent to the servicemen overseas. And since there was a shortage of ingredients, they couldn't make enough for people on the home front. As far as Shirley knew, the only person who had any was Felicia Lieberman. Her father knew someone important in bubble gum, and she had her own private supply hidden away somewhere. But Felicia was stingy and wouldn't give—or sell—a single piece of gum to anyone even if her life depended on it. Once Shirley was willing to go as high as a nickel for a one-cent piece, but Felicia said she couldn't part with any because her supply was dwindling.

Mr. Zelnick, who was behind the prescription

counter, waved to them. His son, Manny, was busy working the soda fountain. When he saw Shirley and Morton walking toward him, he called out, "Two chocolate malteds coming up."

Shirley paused for a moment to tuck her shirt back into her slacks. Then she made her way to the wooden soda fountain, where Manny, blue-eyed and sandy-haired, stood in his white apron and little white hat.

"How did you know what we wanted, Manny?" She resisted the urge to plunk herself down on the stool as she usually did. Instead, she lowered herself onto it easily and crossed her legs. Maybe this was the way Lana Turner had been sitting when she was discovered at a soda fountain in Hollywood.

"Summer's here, your first day of vacation. I had a pretty good idea," said Manny, reaching for two metal containers.

That was so like Manny. He really understood kids. Maybe that's because he just got finished being a kid himself, Shirley thought. Fresh out of high school, he was the only grown-up—or almost grown-up—who ever bought lemonade at Shirley and Morton's lemonade stand. He was the only one who bought comic books at their comic-book stand—even though he had a drugstore full of comic books. Manny was the one who had patiently explained the bubble gum situation to Shirley when she had complained to him.

Shirley had always looked forward to coming to Zelnick's for malteds. But lately she wasn't sure if it was the malteds that brought her here. Or Manny.

"I'll make them extra thick for you," Manny said. He glanced at Mr. Zelnick and flashed Shirley and Morton a smile. "But don't tell the boss."

Shirley inhaled the delicious chocolate, vanilla, and strawberry smells that hovered around the soda fountain. Then she gazed at Manny and studied the way he filled the containers with ice cream, chocolate syrup, milk, and Horlicks malt. He attached the containers to the mixers and started the motor. When he turned around and caught her eye, she glanced away.

"Mmm, I can't wait," said Morton, and he spun himself around on the stool. Shirley had forgotten all about him. She uncrossed her legs because it was uncomfortable to sit that way. Then she found herself spinning around with him.

Shirley and Morton stopped spinning just as the mixers stopped mixing. Two packets of cookies, two empty glasses, and two straws apiece were already on the counter in front of them. And then came the moment they had been waiting for. Manny poured the thick, foamy malteds into their glasses, with plenty left over in the containers for second helpings.

"How's that?" Manny asked.

But there were no answers. Shirley and Morton were happily sipping away.

"I won't be around here to make malteds for you much longer," Manny said.

Shirley came up for air. "Why not, Manny? Are you getting fired?" She laughed at her own joke, playing for time. She didn't want to hear that he was going anywhere. She bit into a cookie and waited for his answer.

Manny grinned and began wiping up the marble counter with the towel that was wrapped around his waist. "I'm joining the army."

Morton's head jerked up, and the straws almost fell out of his mouth. "Wow! The army? No kidding?"

"Really, Manny?" Shirley asked.

"Really and no kidding," Manny said. "In just a few weeks, I'll be one of Uncle Sam's nephews." He saluted.

"What did you do? Enlist?" Morton asked.

"Sure did," said Manny. "I couldn't help it. I saw one of those posters that said UNCLE SAM WANTS YOU. And he was pointing straight at me. What else could I do?"

"You could've waited until they drafted you,"

said Shirley, placing the unfinished cookie on the counter.

"Hey, don't look so worried. I won't be going for a couple of weeks yet. And then I have all that basic training before they ship me out. We'll still have time for a few malteds before I go." He gave them another salute and went off to wipe up the rest of the counter.

"Wow!" Morton said again as he and Shirley walked back home toward Thirteenth Street. "Is Manny ever lucky. I wish I was old enough to join up and go overseas."

"Maybe Manny won't get sent overseas," said Shirley. "Maybe the war will be over by the time he finishes his basic training." She was missing him already. It seemed to her that she was missing lots of people lately. Besides her third-cousin Marine, she also had a cousin in the navy and one in the army air corps. And they were first cousins, too.

Shirley's mother often baked cookies for them. And even though Shirley wasn't much interested in baking, when it came to her cousins, she enjoyed helping. Sometimes they even sent along warm socks and gloves in the packages. Now Shirley would bake cookies for Manny, too. And send him warm socks and gloves.

As they passed the apartments on Independence, they looked for the small white flags hanging in some of the windows. Each flag displayed one or two blue stars, indicating the number of family members serving in the armed forces.

"There's a new one." Morton pointed to a flag displayed in the window of a second-floor apartment.

"That makes four flags on this street alone," said Shirley. Soon Mr. Zelnick would have one of those blue-starred flags hanging in his window. She began to imagine Manny, looking so handsome in his soldier uniform. Although he'd look even more handsome in a sailor uniform, she thought. And if he was in the navy, he could send her a sailor hat, which was what she'd been wanting since the war began, practically. But what she really wanted was for the war to be over by the time Manny was ready to go. If only she could do something to help the war effort.

"I wish we could do something important to help win the war," she said.

"There's got to be a million things we could do," said Morton.

"Like what?"

"I don't know. We'll have to think about it."

They reached the empty lot and went through it, kicking old cans and rocks along the way. In April, during clean-up week, Shirley and Morton and a few other kids had decided to clean up the lot. But it turned out to be more work than they had bargained for, and they quit after thirty minutes.

"I hope we do a better job on the war than we did on the lot," Shirley said, and she began reciting the poem she had written for clean-up week:

> Mother Nature does her share
> To give our city the best of care.
> With her sun and with her rain,
> The flowers soon will bloom again.
> The grass—

"*Again* doesn't rhyme with *rain,*" Morton interrupted.

"The endings are spelled the same," said Shirley.

"But they don't rhyme."

"They do if you say *a-gain.*"

"Nobody says *a-gain.*"

"President Roosevelt does."

That was the end of the argument. Nobody on Thirteenth Street ever disagreed with President Roosevelt.

· 2 ·

Shirley and Morton lived right next door to each other on the first floor of a three-story apartment building, the back of which faced the empty lot. Their apartments shared the same back porch, which was divided by a short partition. They shared a common stairway, which led right down to the sidewalk that bordered the empty lot.

There were seven stairs, and at last count, Shirley could jump over four of them. There was no point in walking down stairs when you could jump them. And now, on this first day of vacation, as Shirley was climbing up these stairs two at a time, she could hear the sound of the radio coming from her apartment.

". . . Our Gal Sunday . . . the story of an orphan girl named Sunday from the little mining town of Silver Creek, Colorado . . ."

Mrs. Cohen was in the kitchen, ironing. Her dark hair was pulled back in a bun, and little beads of perspiration dotted her nose and forehead.

". . . The story that asks the question—can this girl from a mining town in the West find happiness as the wife of a wealthy and titled Englishman? . . ."

"They're always asking that question," Shirley said as she slammed the screen door behind her. "You'd think they'd know the answer by now."

"Without the question, there wouldn't be any story," Mrs. Cohen explained. "How was your malted?"

Shirley licked her lips. "Mmm, delicious." At least it had been before Manny told her about the army. "Can I get another one tomorrow?"

"We'll see. How about ironing some of Daddy's handkerchiefs for me? I'm all in."

While Mrs. Cohen poured herself some coffee, Shirley sprinkled water on the handkerchiefs from the small bottle on the ironing board. Then she spread out one of the handkerchiefs on the board and pressed the hot iron against it. Hot metal meeting cold water. She loved the hissing sound it made, and the smell of steam, and the way the wrinkles disappeared.

"Ma, did you hear about Manny Zelnick? He's joining the army."

Mrs. Cohen brought her coffee to the table and sat down to wait for it to cool off. "It seems that everyone's going into the service these days," she said and blew into the cup. "Thank God Daddy's too old to go and Irving's too young."

"Too young for what?" came a voice from the back porch. The voice was immediately followed by the slamming of the door.

Shirley looked up from her handkerchief and saw Irv finish up the last of a cherry Popsicle and dump the stick into the garbage. She could hardly believe that this was the same brother she beat in a race last summer around the Douglas Park Lagoon. That was when Irv was in his fat year. Now he was tall, slim, handsome, and going into eighth grade.

"We were just being thankful," said Mrs. Cohen.

Shirley finished the rest of the handkerchiefs and set the heel of the iron on the ironing board. "There, I'm all done."

"Good," said her mother. "Now how about helping me straighten up the house a little?"

"What? Work on my vacation?"

"Don't you think I could use a little vacation, too, sometimes?"

That was one of those questions Shirley didn't have an answer for. And there was another question she didn't have an answer for. Why was it fun to clean up for your teacher but work to clean up for your mother?

"Can I straighten up a little later on?" Shirley asked. "I just came in for a few minutes while Morton went to the bathroom. I have to go back out and meet him. We're going to figure out ways to help win the war."

"For which side?" Irv asked.

"Oh, shut up, Irving. Who's talking to you?"

"Vat vas dat you said? You tell the great Irving to shut up?" And with that, he strode across the kitchen floor, positioned himself behind Shirley, and caught her left arm in a hammerlock.

"Cut it out, Irv. Let me go."

"Say *uncle.*"

"No."

Irv tightened his grip slightly and grunted loudly.

"Ma, tell him to let go," Shirley cried out.

"Irving, please," Mrs. Cohen pleaded in exasperation.

"Not until she says *uncle.*"

"Okay, already. *Uncle.*"

15

"Uncle who?"

"Uncle Irving. Now let go."

Irv released Shirley with an air of victory, and Mrs. Cohen chased them both out of the house while Our Gal Sunday was still waiting to find happiness with Lord Henry Brinthrope.

Out on the porch, Shirley and Irv were greeted by Stinky, a pregnant alley cat that Shirley and Morton had found about a month ago, wandering around the empty lot meowing and looking pathetic. They had fed her smoked fish heads that Mrs. Cohen had thrown into the garbage after supper and had kept her in the basement so she'd have a place to live. But Otto, their new janitor, wouldn't let her stay there. He'd said she smelled up the basement. So they named her Stinky and gave her a home in a cardboard box in the sheltered corner of Shirley's porch.

"Hi there, sweetheart," said Shirley, stooping down to scratch the cat behind her ears. Stinky closed her eyes and began to purr.

She and Morton hadn't known Stinky was pregnant when they found her. But soon after, they noticed how she began to bulge out at the sides, getting fuller and rounder each day. They thought it was because of all the food they were feeding her. But Mrs. Cohen had remarked, "If you ask me, she's expecting kittens."

"She sure is getting big," said Irv, reaching down to pet the cat. "I wonder how many kittens she's gonna have."

"She'd better have them soon," said Shirley. "It's going to be hard for her to carry them around in the heat."

"It's good you've got her box in the shade. Just make sure you always keep her water dish filled."

Shirley liked having this serious conversation with her brother. It didn't happen too often. He was usually too busy teasing her.

"I wonder what the kittens will look like," Shirley said. "I wonder if they'll be gray-striped like Stinky or look like the father, whoever he is."

"You spend so much time with her, they'll probably look just like you," Irv said. He gave her a shove and made a dash for the stairs.

"Jerk!" Shirley called after him as he ran into the alley. She carefully picked Stinky up and held her. "Don't pay any attention to him," she told the cat. "Your kittens will be beautiful, no matter who they look like." She gave her a hug and set her back down on the porch.

Shirley ran down the steps to join Morton, who was walking around the old abandoned garage that sat at the edge of the lot next to the alley. For as long as Shirley could remember noticing stray dogs and cats around Thirteenth Street, it had been a dream of hers to clean up the garage someday and make it a home for them. But for as long as she could remember, there had been a rumor that the garage was inhabited by rats. It was old and decrepit and spooky-looking. And neither Shirley nor any of the other kids could ever work up the courage to go inside. Nobody, it seemed, even the adults, wanted anything to do with it.

Morton was picking up stones and sniffing them. Shirley ran over to him. "What are you smelling for, Morton?" She picked up a stone and threw it at a telephone pole across the alley. Bull's-eye.

"I'm smelling for cheese. Some stones smell like cheese. This one, for instance." He held out a yellowish stone to her. "It looks like cheese, doesn't it? And it smells like cheese, too." He stuck the stone under Shirley's nose. "See what I mean?"

"You're right. It does smell like cheese."

Morton placed the stone on the ground near the hole in the garage, which was said to be a rathole, though Shirley and Morton had never seen a rat go into it or come out of it.

"When the rat smells this, I bet he'll come out of the hole," Morton said.

They searched for more stones that smelled

like cheese to improve their chances of seeing a rat, and then they sat on the steps to wait and watch. The only sign of life was Howie Jacobs walking toward them from across the alley.

Howie was a skinny kid with straight brown hair. He was also very smart. Not only was he smart, but he wore glasses, which made him *look* smart. He read newspapers all the time. Not just the comic strips, but the news, too. Howie was the only person Shirley knew who actually liked school and would never even think of ditching. He sat down on the bottom step. "What's everyone doing?" he asked.

"Watching for rats," Morton said.

"And trying to think of ways to help win the war," Shirley added.

"There's lots of ways," Howie said. "You can collect old newspapers like we did in school, and collect tin cans because the country needs lots of tin, and collect meat fats for ammunition, and—"

"And plant a victory garden," Shirley burst in. "President Roosevelt wants everyone to plant victory gardens. People have been planting them all over the country, ever since the war started. We should, too."

"Sure. There's tons of things to do."

Shirley shot up from the step. "Hey, I've got an idea. Let's start a club and do all those things."

She was so excited now she forgot about the rats.

"That would make the hundredth time we started a club," Morton said. "We always start them and finish them the same day."

"That's because we never had a reason for a club before. Now we do. We have a club to help bring victory to America. A victory club!" *Victory.* How she loved that word. If they could help bring victory to America and end the war, they could bring her cousins and Manny home sooner.

"We'll get Donnie to join, too," Howie said.

"And Marilyn," Shirley added. Marilyn was Marilyn Schatz, and she was Morton's cousin.

"Not Marilyn," Morton said.

"Why not Marilyn?" Shirley asked.

"She's a girl."

"Hey, so am I."

"You're different."

Shirley considered for a moment and decided to take this as a compliment. She *was* different from the other girls she knew, who always acted the way girls were expected to act. Like Marilyn Schatz, who played house and jumped rope and took elocution lessons to learn good speaking habits. Or the ones who ran and threw like typical girls and never scraped their knees. She didn't want to be like them. Or dress like them, either. Even when she had been small, she wouldn't wear frilly dresses or put bows in her hair or carry cute little red-and-white purses.

Those girls didn't know the fun they were missing. Shirley lived a life of action, adventure, and excitement as the neighborhood tomboy. She could outrun any boy on the block; throw, catch, and bat a ball as well as any of them; and beat them all at marbles. Shirley's neighbors often joked that she was one of the boys. And it was true. She knew how to have fun. And by the end of summer, she'd have her scabs to prove it.

"Marilyn always comes around here. It wouldn't be fair to keep her out of the club," Shirley said.

"Yeah. Okay. My mother will make me ask her anyway."

"We can start with the victory garden," Shirley suggested.

"Yeah," said Morton. "We can use that piece of ground under my window. And you've got all those seeds you sent away for."

Leave it to Morton to remind Shirley of the twenty-five packets of seeds she had ordered from the back cover of a comic book. "Easy to sell," the ad assured her. "At just ten cents a packet, all your friends, neighbors, and relatives will want them."

Well, none of her friends, neighbors, and relatives had wanted any. Now Shirley had twenty-five packets of seeds she didn't know what to do with, and she still owed two dollars and fifty cents to the seed company. And until she sent in the money, she had no way of getting the prize she wanted. It was a toss-up between a wood-burning set and a shuffleboard.

"They're mostly flower seeds," Shirley told Morton. "The only vegetables they sent are carrots and radishes."

"That's good," Howie said. "They grow fast. My mother once planted some at the side of our building, and they came up real quick."

"But I don't like carrots and radishes," said Shirley, who was thinking more along the lines of cucumbers and sweet corn.

"Me neither," said Morton.

"So what?" Howie said. "As long as they grow fast. We won't have to wait long for the stuff to come up."

"You're right," said Shirley. She was willing to make sacrifices for her country—though she wasn't quite sure how victory gardens with their carrots and radishes could help win the war. But it didn't matter. If that's what President Roosevelt wanted her to do, she was prepared.

Shirley started up the steps, two at a time, to the porch and then turned to face Morton and

Howie. "We're having watermelon tonight. Anyone want to spit seeds over the rail?"

"Maybe," said Howie.

"Sure," said Morton. "And let's save some seeds for the victory garden. We'll grow our own watermelons."

"Can watermelons really grow in Chicago?" Shirley asked, thinking that they needed a sunny climate, like California or Florida. It was fun buying watermelons from the peddler who parked his horse and wagon in the alley, but it would be even more fun to grow their own.

Howie shrugged. "I don't know, but it's worth a try."

Watermelon. Shirley glanced at the plot of ground under Morton's window, imagining their victory garden in full bloom, with red, ripe melons. She was feeling happier by the moment. Watermelons were much more exciting than carrots and radishes.

◦ *3* ◦

The apartment Shirley lived in consisted of four rooms: a kitchen, a dining room, a front room, and one bedroom, which she shared with Irv. Her mother and father slept on a hideaway bed in the dining room. During the day the bed could be folded up and turned into a couch.

Most of the time Shirley didn't mind sharing a room with Irv, but sometimes she wished she could have more privacy. It would be so nice to be able to get dressed and undressed in the bedroom instead of in the bathroom. Or walk around the bedroom in her underwear. Lately she had been wanting her privacy more and more than ever. She was becoming embarrassed by the small, rounded bumps that were beginning to show through her polo shirts.

Her mother had told her that she was becoming a young lady. That she was beginning to develop. Shirley hated it when her mother talked to her like that. *Young lady. Develop. Develop* was an okay word for what you did with film. But it was not okay for what was happening to her breasts. Another word that she didn't like to hear.

Shirley was not ready to develop. If only she could stop those bumps from growing for a while. Or at least hide them. Even with the larger polo shirts she had begun wearing, they still showed. How could she be one of the boys when bumps were showing through her shirts?

After Shirley dusted the furniture and swept the rugs with the carpet sweeper, she decided that she had done enough straightening up for the day. She went into the bedroom to check on her seeds. She kept them hidden in the bottom drawer of her dresser, beneath her underwear, so Irv wouldn't see that she hadn't sold any. He had told her, when she first ordered the seeds, that she wasn't going to sell any, and now she didn't want him to know that he was right.

Also in the drawer was the Brownie camera her mother and father had given her for her eleventh birthday a few weeks ago. Next to it was the envelope of pictures that had been developed from the roll of film that was shot that day. Shirley sat cross-legged on the floor and looked at them. Most were close-up shots of Irv's face, or parts of it. He had grabbed the camera away from her and had kept taking pictures of himself. And even though she had been angry with him for doing that, now she couldn't help but laugh at the blurry shots of his nose, teeth, or the top of his head. Sometimes he even managed to get his whole face in.

She came to one of her and Irv. Irv's hands were around Shirley's throat, and he was sneering into the camera. Shirley's tongue was lolling out the side of her mouth. She remembered how she had tried for a cross-eyed effect. But she came out looking popeyed instead.

There was a picture of her holding Stinky in her arms. The cat was looking straight at the camera, as if she knew she was having her picture taken. Shirley's hair was neatly braided, and her striped polo shirt was tucked into her jeans. She was smiling what her mother called her Mona Lisa smile.

In another picture, Shirley, Morton, Marilyn, Howie, and Donnie were standing on the porch with their arms around each other, laughing or making faces at the camera. Shirley's shirt was now halfway out of her jeans, and her braids were coming apart.

They were great pictures. She decided to take lots more of them this summer. She took the camera out of the drawer and placed it on top of her dresser. Then she looked through her seed packages.

There, among the petunias, zinnias, and nasturtiums, Shirley found her carrots and radishes. Two packets of each. She put them aside to save for the victory garden. She looked at the other twenty-one packets and came to the conclusion that she would never sell them. Every spring, some of Shirley's neighbors planted flowers in window boxes or in flower boxes on their back porches. These were the people Shirley had hoped to sell to. But she was too late. By the time the seeds had arrived, a few weeks ago, her neighbors and everyone else she asked had either finished planting or just weren't interested. Shirley knew that if she wanted her prize, she would have to pay for it herself.

She found the comic book and looked again at the back cover, at the smiling faces of all the satisfied customers who had sold not just twenty-five packets of seeds but even fifty or a hundred, and received fabulous prizes. Shirley decided that they were all phonies and probably hadn't sold any either. They probably bought all the seeds themselves; either that, or the company was lying.

After looking over all the prizes, she finally chose the shuffleboard. The wood-burning set might be dangerous. Maybe she would get burned—or electrocuted. And besides, the Victory Club could play shuffleboard after the meetings.

Very carefully and neatly, Shirley filled out the coupon on the back cover of the comic book and checked the box next to where it said *shuffleboard*. Then she found her dime bank and emptied it out on her bed. She was counting the dimes when Irv came tap-dancing into the room. He was being Gene Kelly again.

"Hey, I could use some of that," he said as he threw himself onto the bed and scooped up a fistful of coins.

"Come on, Irv, give it back," Shirley said.

"Where did you get all this money, anyway?"

"It's my seed money. I'm sending away for my prize."

"You mean you sold all those seeds you ordered?" He began to toss the dimes back to Shirley one at a time.

"What does it look like?"

"Who did you sell them to?"

"A girl in my class." Shirley didn't think of this as a lie, exactly. She was, after all, a girl in her class.

"What does she want with so many seeds?"

"It just so happens," said Shirley, "that a girl in my class is moving to California." Shirley thought that this was a perfectly good explanation. She always pictured California as a place with lots of flowers. And she figured that anyone moving there might want to take along some flower seeds for planting. Also, a girl in her class really was moving to California.

Irv tossed the rest of the dimes onto the bed. Then with his finger, he made the circular crazy sign at the side of his head while he tapped his way out of the bedroom.

Shirley counted out twenty-five dimes and put the other fifteen dimes back into her bank. It had taken her over two months to collect all these dimes. Whenever she had a spare dime, she put it into her bank.

She taped the dimes to a piece of paper and enclosed it in an envelope with the coupon. She would get a three-cent stamp from her father and mail the envelope after supper. Right now, though, there was something else that she wanted to do.

Shirley went to the bedroom window and looked out onto Thirteenth Street. It was a quiet street, with a tall elm tree that stood guard in front of her apartment building. Near the tree, facing each other, were two benches where the old people sat on warm summer evenings. Across the street there was another building very much like the one Shirley lived in.

Shirley looked up and down the street to see if Simone Schwab and her boyfriend Alvin were necking in a parked car. Simone and Alvin and some of the older kids on the block often sat in cars, talking and kissing, and Shirley loved to watch them. How she tingled whenever she saw them necking. And how strange that she never felt that way at any other time. She often wondered why.

She was afraid, too. Afraid that Simone or Alvin would catch her in the act. That they would look up at the window and see her there. But she enjoyed the pleasant sensations that ran through her when she watched, so she kept on doing it. Sometimes when she watched, she wished she had a pair of binoculars so she could zero in on them. She liked to count to see how long they could hold a kiss before they needed to take time out for breathing. Once she counted up to twenty-one, and she was counting slowly, too.

No one was parked on Thirteenth Street today. Maybe it was too hot out for kissing. All she saw was Otto the janitor watering the grass in front of the apartment building.

Otto was a tall man who always wore bib overalls. He lived in a basement apartment at the other end of the building, and Shirley and Morton were very suspicious of him. He didn't speak much, but when he did, it was with an accent. And it wasn't the Yiddish accent they were so used to hearing in their neighborhood either. It was German, definitely. Shirley saw enough war movies to recognize a German accent when she heard one. In these movies, the Germans were always talking about how they were the Master Race and how Hitler would lead them in conquering the whole world.

Although Otto didn't do much talking, he did a lot of watching and listening. He watched the kids play—with too much interest, Shirley thought. And she was convinced, by the way he seemed to tilt his head in their direction, that he listened in on people's conversations. Of course, he always pretended to be working, but Shirley knew he was really watching and listening.

Now he was watching Stinky the cat as she snuck up on a robin taking a bath in the wet grass in front of her building. What a crazy cat. She was always sneaking up on birds, even though Shirley had never seen her catch any. Maybe she was too pregnant to move quickly. She looked as if she were ready to pop at any moment.

As Shirley watched, she realized what a really ugly cat Stinky was. Dull gray stripes, with a head that seemed too small for the rest of her. And, except for her rounded belly, she still had that scrawny look, no matter how much they fed her. Maybe it was because the cat was so ugly that Shirley loved her so much. If she and Morton hadn't given her a home, probably no one else would have.

Stinky snuck up closer and closer to the robin and finally made her grand leap. She missed as usual and got caught in the spray from Otto's hose. Otto laughed at the sight of poor Stinky running off to find a dry place for herself. Shirley couldn't see what was so funny. Otto had probably sprayed her on purpose.

Shirley watched from the window as the blue Dodge pulled up in front of the building. Her father was home from work. Harry Cohen owned the Atlas Mattress & Bedding company. It was a small company, but her father was the boss, and that made Shirley feel proud. Especially when his truck made deliveries to the neighbors who bought Atlas mattresses. The driver always parked the truck in the empty lot next to the alley, and Shirley got to sit in the driver's seat or climb into the back of the truck or do anything she wanted to. After all, her father was the boss, and that made her the boss, too, sort of.

Mr. Cohen exchanged a few words with Otto and then pulled a package out of the car. Shirley couldn't imagine what it could be. Her father sometimes brought home boxes of yellow string and mattress buttons for her and Irv to tie together for use in the mattresses Mr. Cohen manufactured. Irv liked to kid him about the cheap labor he was getting away with and how he was violating child-labor laws. But this package was much too large to be string and buttons.

Shirley ran out of the bedroom and met her father as he opened the front door.

"Hi, Daddy. What's in the package?"

"Material for your mother," Mr. Cohen said, and he handed the package to Mrs. Cohen, who came to greet him.

"Oh, phooey," said Shirley, who couldn't imagine anything more boring than material. "I was hoping it might be a sailor hat. Or a year's supply of Dubble Bubble. Anyway, why are you bringing material home all of a sudden? Ma always buys hers at Sears Roebuck." Shirley had memories of long hours spent waiting at Sears while her mother picked out her patterns and materials. The store always seemed to be boiling, and sometimes she felt as if she would suffocate from lack of air. If Irv was with them, he would grasp his throat and pretend to be choking to death right there in the middle of the satins and velvets.

"I received a special order for casket linings," said Mr. Cohen. "Ma is going to sew them up for me."

Irv got up from the dining room floor, where he had been listening to the radio. "Casket linings? Sounds gruesome."

"You can say coffin linings, if that sounds better," said Mr. Cohen.

"That's even worse," said Shirley, and she gave a little shiver. They were both gruesome words. She didn't want to hear about anything that had to do with death and dying.

"There comes a time for everyone," her mother had often said after she heard that someone had died. Everyone. That meant Shirley's grandparents, who were getting old. It meant her mother and father one day. And a very long time from now, it would mean her. And Irv. She couldn't bear to think of any of it. She shivered again.

Shirley was glad when her mother served supper so she could change the subject from casket linings to the Victory Club. There was a war on, after all, and the sooner they helped end it, the better. So soldiers wouldn't have to come home in caskets that someone had lined.

"You know," said Shirley as she cut into a piece of meat, "the first thing we're going to do is plant a victory garden." She tried to separate the meat from the fat, but she had a hard time finding edible pieces.

"You're picking," said her father.

"There's too much fat on this meat."

"Meat has to have fat."

"It's the best I could do," her mother added. "You shouldn't complain. We're lucky to have it."

"But I hate fat," said Shirley.

Her father gave her an exasperated look. Shirley hoped that he and her mother wouldn't start telling her about wasting food and the starving children in Europe. She knew all about that, and she felt bad for the children. She didn't want them to starve, and she'd be more than happy to give them her meat and fat if she could.

"Think of the starving children in Europe," said Irv.

Shirley gave him the same kind of look that her father had given her, but she also noticed that Irv had hidden his fat under his mashed potatoes.

She wanted to bring back the subject of the victory garden. Even though she had never understood how planting gardens helped the war effort, she wanted to know the reason now. She'd ask about it in a casual way, so as not to appear stupid.

"A victory garden is important, don't you

think?" Shirley said as she poured herself some Old Colony cream soda and sipped.

"Every little bit helps," said her mother.

"But how does it help, exactly?" She continued sipping, hoping she was appearing casual.

"I can't believe you don't know," said Irv. "The reason is simple. When our planes run out of bombs, we can drop tomatoes on the Germans and Japs."

"Stop acting stupid," said Shirley. She was anxious to hear what her mother had to say.

"Who's acting?" asked Irv, flicking a pea-sized mashed-potato ball at her.

"Much of what our farmers grow we send to our boys overseas," Mrs. Cohen offered.

Shirley had always liked that expression—*our boys overseas.*

"And that makes a shortage here. So it helps if people on the home front grow their own vegetables."

So that was it. Shirley liked knowing that by growing her own carrots, radishes, and maybe watermelons, they wouldn't have to buy any, and there would be more to send to—our boys overseas.

Through the window, Shirley saw Stinky sitting on the ledge, peering into the kitchen. Then she saw old Mr. Kaluzna, their neighbor who shared the other side of the porch, walking by with his bottle of seltzer. A few seconds later, she heard a knock on the screen door, and he walked in.

Without a word, he walked over to a shelf, pulled out two glasses, set them in front of her mother and father, and squirted seltzer into them. Then he sat down at the table to keep them company. Mrs. Cohen cleared the dishes and served them all watermelon.

"So, Cohens, what's new?" Mr. Kaluzna asked.

Shirley got up to scrape the dishes so she could save the scraps for Stinky, while Irv sat and listened to their parents and Mr. Kaluzna discussing the war. There was a lot to talk about ever since D-Day, two weeks earlier, when the Allies had invaded Normandy.

"Well, we're winning on both fronts," said Mr. Kaluzna. "Europe and the Pacific. We're mopping up the Germans and the Japs."

Shirley wondered which front Manny would be sent to.

"Yes, but at what cost to our own boys?" said Mrs. Cohen. "Fifteen hundred killed last week in Saipan alone. And God knows how many in the invasion."

"What choice do we have?" asked Mr. Cohen. "We're not the ones who started the war. Germany and Japan did. Better for us to mop them up than the other way around."

"Of course there's no choice," said Mrs. Cohen, getting up to do the dishes and to fight her own personal war with the pots and pans. "This lousy war." *Bang!* "That lousy Hitler—he should drop dead. Germany isn't enough for him." *Bang!* "Now he wants the whole world." *Bang!* "And God knows what's happening to the Jews in Europe. It worries me sick."

Shirley had heard her parents and relatives and her neighbors talk about how Hitler was rounding up Jews from different countries and putting them in concentration camps, where they were being murdered, even little children. If Shirley and her family had been living in one of those countries, Hitler would be after them, too.

"I'm going out to feed Stinky," said Shirley as she wrapped the scraps in a napkin. She didn't want to stay and listen to any more talk about the war and people getting killed.

"Fix yourself up first," said her mother.

"Fix what up?"

"Well, look at you," said Mrs. Cohen as she dried her hands and began tucking Shirley's shirt into her slacks. "You're coming apart."

"I can't help it," said Shirley. "My shirts always come out."

"That's because you don't have a waist yet."

Shirley pictured herself walking around without a waist. She saw an empty space where her waist should've been. On top of the space was her chest, and underneath it were her legs.

She went into the bedroom for her camera and slung it over her shoulder. Back in the kitchen, she picked up the napkin with Stinky's food scraps, plucked two pieces of watermelon from the plate, and walked out the door.

◦ *4* ◦

Shirley watched with pleasure as Stinky gobbled up the meat scraps from her bowl. It always made her feel good to see the cat eating and enjoying her food.

Now there was something else that was making Shirley feel good—taking away the uneasiness she had felt earlier in the kitchen. At first she couldn't put her finger on the reason. Then she realized what it was. Music—lively and energetic—was coming out of the Kaluznas' apartment and bouncing across the porch. That wonderful patriotic music that played on the radio so often these days. She began to sing along to "This Is the Army, Mister Jones." Stinky looked up at her for a moment and then went back to her food.

Oh, how Shirley loved the war songs. They made her feel proud to be an American. They made her feel strong—certain that America would win the war soon. Maybe that's why the songs were always being played and sung on the radio and in the movies. Maybe that's why they sang them in school. To give people strength.

She was humming along to "Praise the Lord and Pass the Ammunition" when Morton came out to the porch. He was wearing his leather cap and pilot goggles. Shirley loved the cap. It made her wish again that she had a sailor hat.

"I see that Stinky has just finished her supper," said Morton. Stinky was sitting next to her bowl, licking her paws and washing her face.

"She looks adorable when she does that." Shirley smiled at the cat.

"Guess what we're having for supper tomorrow?"

"What?"

Morton made a face. "Liver."

"Yuck," said Shirley.

"Guess what Stinky's having for supper tomorrow?"

"Liver," they both answered at the same time.

Shirley handed Morton a piece of watermelon, and they went over to the porch rail to eat and spit seeds.

They tried to see who could spit seeds farther. They aimed for the lot, but the farthest they reached was the sidewalk. Most of the seeds landed on the porch or on themselves.

"We're not very good at this," said Shirley, picking a seed off her chin. "We need more practice." They collected a few of the seeds and saved them in their pockets for the victory garden.

"Let's go find Donnie and tell him about the club," said Morton, wiping his mouth on his sleeve and his hands on his jeans. Shirley used her sleeve and slacks, too, to wipe her mouth and hands. Then they climbed over and down Morton's porch to the ground. Shirley let Morton go first, so she could hand him the camera. She didn't want to risk breaking it in the climb. Then she went down after him.

They balanced themselves along the low fence that bordered their future victory garden, confident that they wouldn't fall. After all, they were both wearing shoes with Cat's Paw brand "no-slip" soles and heels.

"Look at this," said Shirley as she held her arms out to the side and put one foot in front of the other. "I'm hardly even trying to keep my balance, and I don't feel the least bit ready to fall."

"Yeah, you really can't slip with Cat's Paw," said Morton, who was balancing behind her. A few seconds later, she heard him laughing. "Hey, look who's walking the fence with us."

Carefully, Shirley turned around and saw Stinky following Morton. "She won't fall, for sure," Shirley said, laughing. "She has real Cat's Paw no-slip soles and heels." Shirley jumped off the fence. "I've got to get a picture of this. She'll probably never do it again." She aimed her camera at Morton and Stinky. "Smile, everyone."

Shirley climbed back up on the fence and had Morton take a picture of her and Stinky. "These will make great summer memories," she said after he snapped the picture.

After some more fence walking, they jumped off and ran into the lot. While Shirley leaned over to tie her shoelaces, Morton bent down to examine something that was sticking out of the ground. "Hey, look at this. I never saw it before. It looks like an old golf tee. I bet this place used to be a golf course a long time ago."

Shirley nodded and smiled. It was fun to think that the old lot was once a golf course, but she doubted that it ever had been. She was sure that it had always been just a plain old empty lot.

They made their way to the alley and took the shortcut to Douglas Boulevard. Shirley and Morton knew every shortcut, every secret passageway in the neighborhood. On Douglas they found the mailbox, and Shirley dropped her envelope down the chute. She had put an extra three-cent stamp on it because it was so heavy from all the coins. Then they headed back to the alley, cutting through yards and passageways until they came to Donnie Rosenberg's basement apartment.

"Hey, Donnie," Shirley and Morton called together.

The kids in the neighborhood usually called for each other. They almost never knocked on doors or rang bells. There was always the risk of meeting parents.

"Hey, Donnie!" This time they hollered. "Come on out."

No answer. It was obvious that Donnie wasn't home.

"Let's go," said Shirley. "He'll probably come to the lot later."

It was well known that the lot had always been the unofficial meeting place for everyone. If you hung around long enough, someone was sure to come by.

"I'll race you home," said Shirley when they reached Independence Boulevard. And, to make sure that Morton wouldn't complain later that she cheated, Shirley gave him fair warning. "On your mark, get set, go!"

Go, go, go! Hit the beaches. The invasion is on! Shirley Frances Cohen to the rescue. Run! Faster, faster. Can't let the Germans get you. Can't let them take over the world. Hurry! Run for cover. That large boulder over there. Quick!

Shirley cut off Independence and raced into the lot toward her building, skidding into the dirt and into Howie Jacobs, who was running to catch a pop-up.

"Hey, Shirley, watch where you're going. You made me miss the ball." He and Donnie had been playing pinner baseball against a brick wall of the building.

"Sorry," she said, dusting herself off. But she wasn't really. What was a game of pinners compared to fighting a major battle?

Morton ran up alongside them, huffing and puffing. "I tripped," he said.

Nearby, Marilyn was bouncing a ball, oblivious to everything that was going on. After every few bounces, she turned her leg over the ball while she sang:

> *M, my name is Marilyn,*
> *My husband's name is Montgomery,*
> *We come from Mississippi,*
> *And on our ship we carry mice.*

Shirley shook her head. Did Marilyn actually enjoy doing that?

"Hey, Donnie," Morton said. "We were just looking for you."

"I've been here since supper," Donnie said. Donnie had the curliest hair Shirley had ever seen. His curls didn't seem to go anywhere. They just sat right on top of his head.

"I told Donnie and Marilyn about the club," said Howie.

Marilyn stopped bouncing the ball. "My Aunt Yetta told me first."

"It figures," Morton whispered to Shirley. "That's my mother's way of making sure Marilyn gets into the club."

"When do we start?" Marilyn asked.

"Right now," said Shirley, and she led the way up the steps to the porch. Shirley and Morton brought out some chairs, which they arranged in a semicircle, and the first meeting of the Victory Club began. Shirley had a pencil ready and a pad of paper from Atlas Mattress & Bedding Co.

"Okay, who wants to be president?" Shirley asked.

Stinky jumped out of her box and ran to join the club. She stood in the middle of the semicircle and meowed.

"Stinky for president," Morton shouted, and the rest of them applauded.

"Sorry, Stinky," said Shirley. "You can't be

46

president. But you can be our official mascot. Okay?"

Stinky jumped up on Shirley, kneaded her paws in her lap, and curled up in a ball.

"Okay," said Shirley, scratching the cat on the back of her neck. "I think Morton should be president. He and I both had the idea of figuring out ways to win the war, and I would rather be the secretary."

"It's okay with me," said Morton.

"This is supposed to be a democracy," Howie said. "We're supposed to have an election."

"You want to waste time with an election when there's a war going on?" Shirley asked.

Howie shrugged. "I don't care. I'd rather be treasurer anyway."

"Good idea," said Shirley. Howie was a genius in arithmetic.

"What about me?" Marilyn asked.

"You can be either vice-president or sergeant at arms."

"I'd like to be sergeant at arms," Donnie put in. "Then I can wear my army shirt with the sergeant stripes on it."

"And I'll be the vice-president," said Marilyn, smiling. She sat up very straight and tried to look official.

On her pad of paper, underneath the words

47

The following delivered in good condition, Shirley wrote the names and offices of each member of the Victory Club, including Stinky. Shirley was glad that the officers had been selected so quickly. Now they could get on with the real business of the club.

The Victory Club decided to meet once a day, and each member would pay two cents a meeting for dues. And the first order of business would be planning for the victory garden.

"We'll start planting first thing tomorrow," said Morton, making his first important announcement as president.

"Do we need permission?" Marilyn asked.

"We already have permission," said Shirley. "From President Roosevelt."

"I mean from Otto," said Marilyn.

"Shh," whispered Shirley, motioning toward the sidewalk.

"It's only Otto, sweeping," said Howie.

"Quiet," said Shirley under her breath. "He might be spying." Of course, it was possible, Shirley admitted to herself, that he might just be sweeping up the watermelon seeds. But they couldn't be sure. Anyway, it was exciting to think they might have a spy right in their own neighborhood. In their own building, yet. A spy disguised as a janitor.

"Why would he be spying?"

"We don't know yet," said Morton. "But he's German. And it's possible that he might have been sent here by Hitler."

"There *are* spies around, you know," said Shirley. "Even President Roosevelt warned about them in a speech one time."

"True," said Howie.

"And remember what the government warns: A slip of the lip can sink a ship."

"We don't have any information that can sink a ship," said Donnie.

"Of course we don't," said Shirley. "But maybe there's someone else around here who does. And he's a big blabbermouth. The point is, we have to be aware."

"I think we better ask Otto for permission, or we'll be in trouble," said Marilyn. "Real trouble."

Stinky, who had been curled up on Shirley's lap the whole time, suddenly jerked her head up. Her fur bristled.

"What's wrong, Stinky?" Shirley asked, drawing the cat closer. And then she saw it—a black cat darting across the lot toward the alley. Shirley had never seen that cat before. She took it as an omen. "Let's ask Otto tomorrow. It's the end of the day, and he's probably tired."

"Then I make a motion to adjourn the meeting," said Howie.

"Wait," said Shirley. "I have to do something first." She gently placed Stinky on the floor and ran into her apartment. She came back out again with Irv.

"Okay, Irv," she said, swinging the camera up over her shoulder and handing it to him. "Just take a picture of us. I want to keep a record of our first meeting."

She picked Stinky up and sat down with the cat on her lap. Irv aimed the camera at himself, grinned, and took a picture of his face.

"Come on, Irv. Quit fooling around."

Irv then aimed the camera at the semicircle and peered through the lens. "Everyone say *cheese.*" The members of the club all said *cheese* and smiled. Even Stinky looked up at the camera.

"Good," said Shirley, taking the camera from him. "I'm going to keep a record of this whole summer."

"Okay," said Howie. "I now make another motion to adjourn the meeting. Who seconds?"

"I second," said Donnie.

"Meeting adjourned," said Morton.

Shirley didn't feel that "Meeting adjourned" was a proper enough way to end the first meeting of the Victory Club. She lifted Stinky off her lap and set her on the porch. Then she stood up and began singing "Praise the Lord and Pass the Ammunition." Ever since she heard it coming from the Kaluznas' apartment, the song had been playing inside her like a record on the Victrola.

Imagining herself starring in a war movie, she belted out the song the way Kate Smith did when she sang "God Bless America." A great feeling of pride burst right out of her as she sang. This was, after all, what the Victory Club was all about. Soon Morton joined her, and then the other members. They sang and marched around the porch and down the steps, with Stinky following, past Otto, who was still sweeping the sidewalk, into the empty lot.

Praise the Lord and pass the ammunition,
Praise the Lord and pass the ammunition . . .

"Sha!" Mrs. Lasky called down from the third floor. "Too much noise already."

Mrs. Lasky was a nice old lady. But she had no patience for noise or children. Shirley didn't pay any attention to her. Neither did the others. It wasn't their fault if Mrs. Lasky didn't have any patriotic spirit.

But the members of the Victory Club were filled with patriotic spirit as they continued their

51

march across the lot toward Independence. Oh, if they only had a flag. Then they would be just like the real parades that sometimes marched along the boulevard.

Praise the Lord and pass the ammunition!
Praise the Lord and pass the ammunition . . .

To Shirley there seemed to be a magical power in the words they were singing. And she believed with all her heart that, by singing the song, this power would stretch across the oceans and reach out to our boys overseas.

Praise the Lord and pass the ammunition!
Praise the Lord and pass the ammunition!
Praise the Lord and pass the ammunition,
And we'll all stay free!

○ **5** ○

Shirley woke up the next morning to the sound of the sewing machine in the dining room. Her mother was probably sewing up those gruesome casket linings. The thought of someone making casket linings in your very own house was not the most pleasant one to wake up to. Neither was the thought of having to ask Otto for permission to plant the garden. Shirley buried her face in her pillow. Maybe she would just go back to sleep. On the other hand, the thought of maybe getting another malted at Zelnick's and seeing Manny was a very pleasant one to wake up to. She leaped out of bed.

Irv was still asleep, with his pillow over his head. It would take more than a sewing machine to wake him up. Probably a mine explosion wouldn't even do it.

Shirley took out a pair of Levi's from the

drawer and a polo shirt that had once been Irv's and went into the bathroom to get dressed. Was it her imagination or were her bumps bigger today than they had been yesterday? She quickly covered them up with the shirt.

Next came the Levi's. They were still stiff, even though her mother had washed them about half a dozen times to get the newness out of them. Levi's were not supposed to look new, even when they were. Still, she loved the feel of them. And they were boys' Levi's, too. Not plain girls' jeans like Marilyn Schatz wore when she wasn't wearing dresses.

Shirley was the only girl she knew who wore boys' jeans. People called her a tomboy when she wore them, and she liked that. She had even asked the kids to call her Frankie because of her middle name, Frances. Like Frank Sinatra, who was really Francis Sinatra. When the older girls, the bobby-soxers, swooned over his singing, they didn't sigh, "Oh, Francis." They sighed, "Oh, Frankie." The name Frankie was much cuter than the name Shirley. But Morton had said that Shirley looked more like a Shirley than a Frankie, and the other kids agreed.

She stuffed the packets of seeds into her back pockets and went into the dining room. "Hi," she called to her mother above the noise of the sewing machine.

"You're just in time," said Mrs. Cohen. "I need you to try this on."

What her mother was sewing was almost as bad as casket linings. She was sewing a dress for Shirley. Shirley hated dresses, especially when she had to try them on.

"Do I have to?" she asked. "I just got dressed. And I have important things to do."

"And I have to finish this if you want something new to wear for the High Holidays."

"But Rosh Hashana isn't until September."

"I still have my suit to do and all those casket linings. Everything takes time."

"But we wanted to plant our garden early— before it gets too hot. It's not healthy to work in the heat. You don't want me to get polio, do you?"

"God forbid," said her mother. "I wish they would find a way to prevent it already. A vaccine or something. Like they have for smallpox."

"Well, remember the warnings in the newspaper? Stay away from crowds and beaches. And don't exert yourself. Especially when it's hot out."

Mrs. Cohen removed the blue velvet dress from the sewing machine. "I'll tell you what. Just try it on over your clothes so I can get an idea of how it looks. Next time I'll have to be more exact."

Shirley slipped the dress over her head and tried to wait patiently while her mother pinned and measured. She scratched a mosquito bite on her arm and one on her leg. Everything seemed to itch her when she was being fitted for clothes.

"Hold still," said Mrs. Cohen.

Shirley shifted her weight from one foot to the other. "Ma, do you think we need to ask Otto for permission to plant the garden?"

"It would be nice," said her mother.

"Nice, maybe. But do we have to?"

"I think so."

"Shouldn't we ask the landlord instead?"

"I hardly know the landlord. All we do is send him the rent. I think Otto would be the one to ask."

Shirley wanted to ask her mother if she thought Otto was a German spy, but she couldn't just come right out and say it. What if he wasn't? She'd feel foolish. And the landlord certainly wouldn't hire a spy janitor, would he? But what if he didn't know he was a spy? What if nobody knew?

"Ma, what do you know about Otto?"

"Not much. He hasn't been here that long. But he seems like a nice, quiet man."

"You shouldn't be fooled by that," said Shirley. "It's the quiet ones you have to watch out for." Shirley had once heard Simone Schwab say that. Shirley and her family had been in the park on Independence one evening, and Shirley was eavesdropping on a conversation between Simone and her girl friend, who were lying on a blanket next to them. They were talking about boys.

"I would love to go out with him," the friend had said. "He's just my type. Cute and quiet."

And Simone had answered, "It's the quiet ones you have to watch out for."

Shirley figured that the same could be true of janitors.

"I'm not sure I understand what you're talking about," said her mother, tucking in the material along the sides of the dress and pinning it.

"I mean, here's this guy who you don't know anything about, and all of a sudden he turns up in our building as a janitor. And just because he's quiet, no one worries about him. Who knows what he's up to? He's German. He could be anybody. He could be one of those spies who was landed from a German sub."

"Shirley, you're letting your imagination get carried away."

"Was it my imagination that Uncle Moshe wrote to us from New York saying that people could spot German subs off the coast? And that there was talk that spies were being landed from those subs?"

"That has nothing to do with Otto. He's a good janitor, and he doesn't bother anyone. Don't go jumping to conclusions about him. Let him be."

Shirley could see that there was no point in continuing the conversation. She shifted her weight again. "Are you almost finished?"

"I just want to pin up the hem so I can baste it later." Mrs. Cohen took two pins from the pincushion. She held one in her mouth while she pinned the other to the hem.

"I thought basting is what you did to turkeys."

Mrs. Cohen couldn't talk with the pin in her mouth, so she just rolled her eyes upward.

Shirley wished her mother would hurry up with the hem. Just as it seemed to her that she'd be standing there forever, there was a tapping on the window and a lady calling, "Leo, Leo."

It was Mrs. Kaluzna from next door. She always called Shirley's mother Leo, even though her name was Leah.

"Come in, Sophie," Mrs. Cohen called to her.

"Can I take this thing off now?" Shirley asked, wanting to take full advantage of the interruption.

"All right," her mother said, helping Shirley out of the dress. "I'll finish later. Be careful of the pins."

Mrs. Kaluzna came bustling into the dining room. "Leo, I need your opinion. Which earrings should I wear? The ones with the phony diamonds or the ones with the phony pearls?" She was wearing one of each.

"My, my, look at you," said Shirley's mother. "You're all dolled up."

"Oh, Leo. In this humidity I can't do anything with my hair. It looks like steel wool." Mrs. Kaluzna, her fingers decked with rings that were set with colored stones, plucked at her hair. "See what I mean?" She flashed Shirley a smile.

"Never mind. It looks fine," said Mrs. Cohen.

To Shirley, Mrs. Kaluzna's short, frizzy gray hair did look like steel wool. Still, she looked pretty good for an old lady. She wore a red dress and her white Enna Jettick platform shoes, which she had bought last week on sale for $4.95 at Goldblatt's. Her face was made up with powder, circles of cheek rouge, and red lipstick. She smelled of Evening in Paris perfume, the same perfume Shirley's mother wore every Tuesday night when she went out to her bridge games.

"I have a meeting of the Consumptive Aid Society, and I need your advice about the earrings," Mrs. Kaluzna said.

Without waiting to hear her mother's advice, Shirley went into the kitchen to make herself breakfast. She put some shredded wheat into a bowl and sprinkled a generous serving of sugar on the top.

While Shirley was eating, she studied the lid from the bottle of Capitol Milk. Every bottle had a lid showing a sketch of the Capitol building in Washington and giving the name of a state and its capital. This one was of Illinois. The capital—Springfield. What a gyp. It was her own state capital, and of course she knew the name of it. Shirley was hoping for a more exotic state—like North Dakota. She planned to collect the lids from all forty-eight states. It would be a fun way to memorize all the capitals.

Shirley heard a meowing and turned to see Stinky looking at her through the kitchen window. She poured some milk into a glass and went out onto the porch. As soon as the door opened, Stinky jumped from the window ledge and trotted alongside Shirley to her dish. She began lapping up the milk even before Shirley finished pouring it.

"That's a good girl," Shirley said. "Drink up

all your milk so you'll be big and strong. You're going to be a mommy soon."

Shirley put her hands around the cat's stomach and felt the bulge. "I wonder how many babies you've got inside here. Five or six, I'll bet." She imagined all those kittens bouncing around the porch like furry little balls. She couldn't wait. Although she had no idea what she'd do with all of them once they were born. Who would she give them to?

As Shirley watched Stinky's small pink tongue darting in and out of her mouth, she remembered how hungry the cat had been when they'd found her. She and Morton had wondered how often Stinky had gone without food and promised her that they would never let her go hungry again. They had kept their promise.

"Does it taste good?" Shirley asked the cat.

Stinky looked up from the bowl and licked her mouth.

"Good. I'm glad you're enjoying it."

The cat looked deep into Shirley's eyes and meowed.

"You're very welcome," said Shirley. She petted her for a few minutes and then went next door to Morton's.

Morton was in the kitchen having breakfast. His little brother Harold was sitting in a high chair next to him. Shirley could see and hear them through the screen door. She nonchalantly walked around the porch, whistling and scratching at her mosquito bites, hoping she'd be invited in. Finally Mrs. Kaminsky opened the door.

"Why are you waiting out here by yourself? Come inside. Maybe you can get Harold to drink his orange juice." Morton's mother often went looking for Shirley when Harold didn't want to drink his juice. She held the door open for Shirley. "You know, you don't have to wait for an invitation. You're welcome here anytime."

Shirley knew she was welcome at Morton's house, but she liked hearing it. Mrs. Kaminsky liked Shirley. More than once, she had expressed the hope that one day Shirley and Morton would get married. She never really said it, exactly. She spoke in half sentences. "There's nothing I'd like better than for you and Morton to . . . who knows . . . maybe someday . . ."

Shirley gave Mrs. Kaminsky a smile and sat down at the table next to Harold. Harold was almost two, and Shirley thought he had the most beautiful blue eyes. How she wished she had a baby brother. But whenever she tried talking to her mother about it, her mother changed the subject.

"Hi, Harold," she said. "Guess what? Stinky

just drank all her milk. Boy, will she grow up to be big and strong." She stroked his hair. "Let's see if you can drink all your orange juice, so you'll grow up big and strong, too." She smiled at him.

Harold lifted his glass with both hands, drank the juice, then set the glass down triumphantly. "All gone," he said.

"Good boy," said Shirley.

"Amazing," said Mrs. Kaminsky.

"I'll be finished in a minute," Morton said, stuffing a large piece of bread and jelly into his mouth.

"Stop eating so fast," warned Mrs. Kaminsky. "You'll choke like you did the last time."

Shirley remembered the time Morton choked on a tiny toy whistle that he found as a prize in a package of candy. He tried to blow it, and it went down his throat. The wrong pipe, everyone had said. Morton had told her that his mother had watched for the whistle every time he went to the bathroom.

"I've got the seeds for the garden," said Shirley, tapping her back pockets. Shirley thought that Mrs. Kaminsky would be happy to hear that Morton was planting a garden. His mother had high hopes that he would become a farmer when he grew up. Shirley knew this to be a fact. Many times she had overheard Mrs. Kaminsky telling her mother, "I have high hopes that Morton will go into pharmacy."

But Morton's mother probably wasn't paying attention when Shirley mentioned the garden because she didn't say anything.

Morton took one last gulp of milk, wiped his mouth with his arm, and the two of them went out onto the porch. Stinky ran over to them and rubbed against their legs.

"It's getting warmer," Shirley said. "We should get to work while it's still early." They looked in the direction of Otto's basement apartment.

"I wonder where he is," said Morton.

"His shades are down," said Shirley. "Did you ever notice? His shades are always down in the morning."

"That's probably when he does his spy work," said Morton. "We have to try to get a look in there."

They went over to the steps and sat down, waiting for Otto to appear. They needed his permission, but they weren't quite ready to go looking for him.

Shirley's mother and Mrs. Kaluzna came out to the porch and stood there for a while, talking.

"You're right, Leo. The pearls are better. Not so flashy."

oredom, Shirley and Morton

ters and took turns jumping

tops for both of them.

iddle of one of Shirley's jumps

and she almost toppled down

f steps. He was coming out of

old abandoned garage that, as

uld remember, nobody had ever

And here was Otto, coming out

th a black metal box and closing

y recovered, she and Morton ex-

s. Mrs. Cohen called down from

v are you today, Otto?"

"As always, very busy," said Otto, drawing the metal box closer to his body. "There is always much work to do." He spoke good English in spite of his accent, Shirley noted. Maybe he had gone to a spy school in Germany.

"You are a wonder, the way you fixed my toaster," said Mrs. Kaluzna.

"Otto can fix anything," said Shirley's mother. "He saved my vacuum cleaner. And with parts so hard to get nowadays."

When had Otto fixed their vacuum cleaner? Shirley wondered. She hadn't seen him in her apartment.

"That is my job," he said with a satisfied smile.

"To fix things." And, as if he had just remembered, he turned back to lock the door of the garage.

Shirley wished she had X-ray vision like Superman so she could see what was in the box. And in the garage. She was even more afraid now to ask Otto about the garden. But if she did have to ask, now would be the safest time. While her mother was there, looking down at her from the porch.

Shirley swallowed hard and slowly approached Otto. Up close, he looked even bigger than she thought he was. She motioned for Morton to come with her.

"Is it okay if we plant a garden?" she asked. She did not ask if they could plant a victory garden. Maybe if Otto didn't know it was for victory, he'd be more likely to say yes.

"Just a plain little vegetable garden," Shirley went on. "With some carrots and radishes and maybe watermelons."

"We would use that piece of ground under my window," Morton said, pointing to the place.

They held their breath and waited for an answer. Otto thought for a moment and then nodded. "Yes, if you like, you can plant there."

"Thank you," said Shirley. "Can we use the tools in the basement?" Otto had gardening tools that he used when he worked on the bushes in front of the building. Maybe he would let Shirley and Morton borrow them.

"You can use them. But watch out."

"Watch out?" Shirley and Morton asked.

"The rake is sharp. Very sharp."

Shirley didn't like the way Otto stressed the word *sharp*. Was that a warning?

"We'll watch out," said Shirley, turning toward the basement.

"And we won't break anything either," Morton added.

They hurried away from Otto and ran to the basement.

"Whew," said Shirley, leaning against the door. "That was close."

° **6** °

They rested up for a few minutes, then opened the door. The basement was dark and damp and very scary. Shirley never went in by herself. Only when Morton or Irv or her father went with her would she dare step inside. Unless, of course, her mother was there washing clothes. She liked watching the way the clothes squeezed out of the wringer of the washing machine. And it was interesting to see what kinds of things people kept there—sleds, old baby buggies, and radios. But when she was alone, there was no telling what lurked in the dark corners or inside the sheds.

They were reaching into the air, searching for the light-bulb chain, when something soft brushed up against Shirley's leg. She screamed, "A rat! Morton, help me!"

"What rat? Where?" Morton cried out.

"Meow."

Morton found the chain and turned on the light.

"Oh, Stinky," said Shirley, checking to see if her heart was still beating. "It's only you. You scared us." She picked the cat up and nuzzled her until Stinky leaped out of her arms and jumped into a buggy.

"I'll bet she's looking for a place to have her babies," said Morton.

"A baby buggy is a perfect place to have them," said Shirley. "See what a smart cat she is?"

They found a rake, a spade, and a shovel propped up against the door, along with a beat-up bushel basket. They took them outside so they could immediately begin working.

First they attacked the tall weeds. They tugged and yanked them out of the ground, getting their hands scratched and burned in the process.

"I hope none of this is poison ivy," said Morton, dumping a handful of weeds into the basket.

Shirley began raking up the loose weeds, pebbles, and bottle caps, and chopping at the ground while Morton used the spade to dig up the hard, dry earth. With his foot he pushed the metal blade into the ground and turned over the soil. A grunt accompanied each turn of the spade.

They didn't know what they were doing exactly, never having planted a garden before. But it seemed right—getting rid of the weeds and debris and turning over the earth.

"Hey, look what I found," said Shirley, holding up a small circular object, part metal, mostly rust. "Buried treasure."

"Let me see that," said Morton. He took the object from her and turned it around in his fingers. "Hey, I wondered what happened to this. It's my spinning siren ring. I lost it a couple of months ago. I wonder if it still works." He wiped the ring on his jeans and held it up to his lips.

"You're not going to blow that thing, are you? It's filthy. You could get polio."

He shrugged. "Yeah, maybe I'll wash it off first." He stuck the ring into his pocket and went back to his digging.

Shirley helped him dig with the shovel, pretending she was searching for more buried treasure or trying to reach China, the way she used to when she was younger. It made the time go faster.

Luckily, the plot was a small one. About the size of her dining room table, Shirley figured. The work was getting hard, the morning coolness was deserting them, and they could barely manage the small amount of ground they had. Morton was sweating, and Shirley could see the thin rings of dirt around his neck. Her own damp shirt was sticking to her on all sides.

"Where is everybody?" Morton asked. "Why don't they come and help us already?"

"You can be sure they'll be here in time to help us eat the stuff," Shirley said. She dug the shovel into the earth and turned it over. Dig and turn. Dig and turn. What toil. Why would Mrs. Kaminsky want Morton to be a farmer?

Shirley turned over the last bit of earth just as Marilyn came skipping over, singing "Mairzy Doats." "Am I late?"

"We're almost finished," Morton said. "Where were you?"

"I had to help my mother take down all that disgusting, filthy flypaper hanging from the light fixtures. And then I had to hang up new ones for tonight. You should have seen all those ugly bugs and flies that were stuck to—"

"Here," said Morton, thrusting a branch at her. "You can help us make rows for the seeds."

With the branches, they began making furrows in the ground. Two for the radishes, two for the carrots, and one large one for the watermelons. They planted the seeds according to the directions on the packets, and when they were finished, Morton told Marilyn, "Go ask my mother for my sprinkling can and fill it up with water."

While Marilyn went for the water, Shirley ran into her apartment for her camera. Then she and Morton took pictures of each other in their new garden, among their neat rows, with Popsicle-stick markers stuck through the empty seed packets to identify what was planted where.

"We'll take pictures of the garden as it grows," said Shirley. "So we'll never forget how it looked from the time of planting to the time of harvest." She hugged her camera to her chest and stood there, admiring what they had done and imagining what would be.

Marilyn came down the steps with the sprinkling can, and they took turns watering, being careful not to step where the seeds were planted. Morton sent Marilyn upstairs for a refill.

"There's something I have to do before she gets back," said Morton. Shirley's eyes followed Morton as he walked over to the edge of the garden, next to the building. He stood there for a moment, with his back toward Shirley, and then, of all things, he peed on a spot of earth in the corner of the garden.

"Morton, are you crazy?" Shirley called in a half whisper. "What are you doing that for? Someone might see you."

She looked around uneasily, not understanding why she felt so uncomfortable. Morton had done this kind of thing before. Just this past winter, he wrote his name in the snow, and Shirley thought it was hilarious. She thought it was pretty neat the way boys could do that—write their names on the sidewalk or in the snow. Why, now, was she feeling so embarrassed?

"It's an experiment," Morton said when he was finished. "To see if any watermelon will grow here."

"You could have at least done it on a radish," Shirley said. "You know how I hate radishes." She tried to memorize the exact spot Morton watered, so she'd remember not to eat the watermelon that grew from that seed.

Marilyn came down with the water and an announcement. "Aunt Yetta said we could have Kool-Aid when we're through."

"I'd rather have a malted," said Shirley.

They finished watering and put the tools away in the basement. Howie and Donnie showed up just as they came back out.

"Come on up for some Kool-Aid," Marilyn invited.

"Yeah," said Morton. "You need it after all your hard work on the garden."

"It's not my fault I'm late," said Donnie. "My

ma forgot to wake me. The garden looks swell, though."

"And I was reading the newspaper and forgot what time it was," said Howie. "Did you know that the FBI is still on the lookout for spies and saboteurs?"

"Saboteurs?" asked Shirley. She knew that a spy was someone who passed secret information to the enemy, but she wasn't exactly sure what a saboteur was.

"Yeah. Enemy agents who sneak into the U.S. and try to blow up factories and places and slow down the war effort."

Shirley's eyes met Morton's. She knew they were both wondering the same thing.

"Morton and I saw Otto coming out of the garage today. With a black box."

"What kind of box?" asked Howie.

"It looked like a large toolbox," said Morton. "He's doing something in the garage, all right."

"We'll have to keep an eye on him," said Howie.

"Anyone want to come with me for a malted?" Shirley asked.

"I can't go two days in a row," said Morton. "My ma always worries that I'll get too fat."

Howie and Donnie both said they didn't have

any money on them, and Marilyn had her heart set on Kool-Aid.

Shirley went in to wash up and to get her quarter for the malted. Unlike Morton, she was skinny, and her mother didn't have to worry that Shirley would get fat from drinking too many malteds.

Now, with her laces tied, shirt tucked in—not too tightly because she didn't want her bumps to show—and hair smoothed back, she was ready to go.

She'd walk to Zelnick's this time. Not run. She didn't want to come apart before she saw Manny. She started across the lot, resisting the urge to run, picking up stones and seeing how far she could throw them. She threw one dangerously close to Otto's window. Not to break it. Just to have a reason to look in that direction. His shades were up now. But from that distance, and without lights on in his apartment, she couldn't see anything.

She kicked pebbles across the lot until she reached Independence Boulevard. This walking business was not for her. It felt unnatural. She never walked anyplace when she was alone. It took too long to get where she had to go. She not only liked to run, she needed to run.

Shirley looked down the long stretch of sidewalk that lay ahead and happily came upon a compromise. With arms swinging, she began skipping to Zelnick's. She added a little whistle to her skip. And soon she was whistling and skipping, skipping and whistling, until she found herself in front of the drugstore.

After checking the candy counter for bubble gum, she turned around and spotted Simone Schwab at the soda fountain, draped over the counter, her face just inches away from Manny's. Her chin was cupped in her hands, and her elbow was resting on the counter. What was she doing here with Manny? It wasn't fair. She had Alvin.

Shirley hesitated, then headed toward the soda fountain and sat down two stools away from Simone. Manny looked her way. "Hi, Shirl. Two days in a row. Lucky you." He smiled at her, and Shirley melted like the ice cream that dripped down the sides of Simone's sundae dish.

"Hi," said Shirley, smiling back at him. She placed her quarter on the counter, and Manny reached for the metal container and milk.

Simone slid back onto the stool. She was wearing white shorts to just above the knee and a white off-the-shoulder midriff that revealed lots of tanned skin and covered up more than just bumps. What she had—and Shirley hated to even think the word—were breasts. Real breasts.

One side of her long brown hair cascaded over her right eye, Veronica Lake style. At least it looked like the way the movie star had worn her hair before she pinned it up in braids for the war effort. Too many women had copied her peekaboo style and gotten their hair stuck in machines in the defense plants.

Simone looked Shirley's way. "Shirley—I know you. You're Irv's sister. Cute brother you've got. Too bad he's so young." She took the spoon out of her dish and made a big thing out of licking the ice cream off. "Maybe I'll just wait a couple of years for him to catch up."

Manny set Shirley's malted in front of her just as Simone asked her, "How's your little boyfriend?"

"Little boyfriend?" Shirley asked.

"Yes, you know. What's his name . . . Morton?"

"Oh, Morton. He's fine. How's your boyfriend Alvin?"

Simone gave Shirley a surprised look. "How do you know about Alvin?"

"Uh . . . oh, I see the two of you around sometimes." She quickly went to work on her malted.

"Well, gotta go," said Simone, sliding off the stool. "Remember, Manny, you've got my address. Don't forget to write me." She blew him a kiss.

Shirley imagined herself pouring her malted down Simone's midriff. At the same time, she couldn't help but admire the slinky way in which she moved toward the door, her hips swaying easily from side to side.

"So," said Manny, cleaning up the counter where Simone had been sitting. "Where's Mort?"

"Home, drinking Kool-Aid," said Shirley. "We were both so thirsty after planting our victory garden." She wanted Manny to know that they were doing their part to help win the war.

"Well, don't do too good a job on the garden yet, or I won't even get a chance to go overseas."

"Do you think you'll be sent to the European front or to the Pacific?" She was glad she had listened to the conversation at supper last night.

"I probably won't know until the last minute. When the war first started, when Japan bombed Pearl Harbor, I wanted to fight the Japs. Of course, I was too young then. But now, if I'm gonna fight, I want to fight the Germans. The Master Race." He shook his head slowly. "Some Master Race, huh? Can you imagine them ruling the world? And it's really frightening to think of what's happening to the Jews over there. My mom's got a sister she hasn't heard from since Germany invaded Poland. And that was almost five years ago. So—it's the Germans I want to fight."

"You'll be careful, Manny, won't you?"

"Oh, yeah. Don't you worry about me." He smiled at her again. "You'll come by and see me before I go, won't you?"

"I will," she said. She wanted to add, "I'll write to you" and "I'll be waiting for you." But she didn't. And when she tried to imitate Simone's slinky exit from the drugstore, she couldn't get the slink right. Or the wiggle. Maybe it was because she didn't have a waist yet. Shirley straightened up, walked out the door, and ran home.

° **7** °

In a way, Shirley wanted Manny to leave already. Then she could become the girl he left behind, and she could begin to wait for him. Her daydream began to grow one day as she lay on the dining room couch, listening to the radio playing "You'd Be So Nice to Come Home To."

They'd write letters. At first he'd be happy to hear from her because he was lonely. Then, little by little, he'd begin to realize how much Shirley meant to him. True, she was much younger than he was. But he would be willing to wait for her to catch up. She'd be his girl back home. They'd walk hand in hand along the boulevard or watch boats dock at the harbor on summer evenings and gaze at the sunset together. They'd be sweethearts. In time she'd have—breasts.

She'd even send him a picture of herself that he could tack up onto a wall of his barracks, where the GIs kept pictures of their pinup girls—Lana Turner, Rita Hayworth, Betty Grable. Of course, she wouldn't send him one where her legs showed. Just a snapshot of her from above the shoulders. On second thought, maybe having a picture of her next to all those glamorous movie stars was not such a good idea. She would ask him to carry it with him so he could look at it during the quiet, lonely times in the jungles or on the beaches, or wherever it was that they sent him.

Shirley had always loved those movies about girls and guys in love, separated by war. They were so romantic. And now romance was happening to her as she imagined Manny, lying on his bunk and listening to this same song on Armed Forces Radio and dreaming of coming home to Shirley. She would be his special girl. Chosen above everyone else. Even Simone Schwab.

Oh, she couldn't wait for him to leave.

Shirley turned off the radio and went into the kitchen to help her mother set the table for supper.

"You and Daddy are what—four years apart?" Shirley asked. She was humming the song to herself and placing forks next to the plates.

"Yes," said her mother. "Why?"

"Just wondering." Shirley figured that she and Manny were about seven years apart. Not so impossible. Anything could happen. One day she might even become Shirley Zelnick. The name felt good on her tongue. Shirley Zelnick. Shirl Zelnick. Mrs. Zelnick. She wasn't sure about that last one. It made her sound like she'd be Manny's mother.

After supper, while Shirley was helping her mother with the dishes, Mr. Kaluzna joined her father at the table to discuss the Republican Convention, which had just been held in Chicago.

"So, Harry, it looks like the Republicans have themselves a man." He squirted some seltzer into Mr. Cohen's glass.

"A lot of good it will do them," said Shirley's father, striking a match to light up a Camel cigarette. "Dewey doesn't have a chance against Roosevelt. And there's no question Roosevelt will get the nomination next month." He inhaled and blew the smoke out. "A fourth term. I can't understand why anyone would want that job for so long. To have to carry the problems of the whole world on your shoulders." He shook his head.

"Better him than Dewey. I don't know what it is, but there's something about that man I don't trust."

Shirley didn't like Dewey either. She wasn't exactly sure of the reason. Maybe it was because of his mustache. Or because he was a Republican.

Or maybe it was just because he was running against her President Roosevelt. But, whatever the reason, if she was for Roosevelt, she had to be against Dewey. Phooey on Dewey became her slogan.

Shirley caught a glimpse of Morton through the kitchen window. He was holding an iron and motioning for her to come out. Shirley dried the last of the dishes and ran out to meet him.

"We're in luck," he said to her even before she was out the door. "This iron gets us into Otto's apartment."

"How does it do that?"

He showed her the frayed cord. "My ma wants me to take it to him to fix."

"Well, then, what are we waiting for? It might be our only chance to see what's going on in there." She slid down the banister and waited for Morton to walk down with the iron. They headed toward Otto's apartment at the end of the building.

"Now we just act normal," said Morton. "Like all we're doing is bringing in an iron to fix."

"And meanwhile we get a good look around the place." Shirley's heart quickened as they walked down the steps to the basement and stood in front of Otto's screen door. From inside they heard static sounds and remote voices, which were abruptly cut off after Morton knocked on the door.

A moment later Otto appeared and unlatched the door. His eyes fell upon the iron.

"You have something to fix?" He opened the door for them. "Hurry—before the flies come in."

They stepped into a small kitchen. Smaller than Shirley's and Morton's. But it was very neat. There was not a single glass or dish anywhere in sight. It was an ordinary kitchen, with a stove and refrigerator and a yellow-and-white checkered oilcloth covering the table. Shirley was disappointed. It wasn't anything like the spy kitchen she hoped it would be. At the same time, she had no idea what a spy kitchen was supposed to look like.

Morton was about to show Otto the frayed cord when there was a knock on the door. A man from their building stood outside. "Otto, I hate to disturb you, but I have a small problem at my place."

Otto nodded and walked out to talk with him.

Shirley and Morton gave each other a go-ahead sign by nodding their heads and casually moved around the kitchen, toward the next room. They stood in the doorway and peered into a room barely larger than the kitchen. In the corner, light from a floor lamp lit up a strange-looking radio on a table. It was a large gray metal box with all kinds of controls and dials. It looked nothing like the dark, varnished wooden radio that Shirley had at home.

Morton gave Shirley's arm a jab and whispered to her. "A shortwave radio. I saw one like that in a spy movie."

Shirley pointed to the wall, where a large map was tacked onto a bulletin board. Red, yellow, and blue tacks were stuck into various places on the map. But, except for knowing it wasn't a map of the United States, Shirley had no idea what she was looking at. Even at school she could never make any sense out of the maps they studied during geography. Once, when she was in the third grade, her teacher asked her which way was north. And Shirley, thinking of the top of the map, had answered, "Up." The teacher had said she was wrong. North, she told her, was in the direction of the North Pole.

". . . first thing tomorrow," Otto was saying. Shirley and Morton turned around quickly and moved away from the doorway.

"Now," said Otto, coming toward them. "Let me see what you have." He took the iron from

Morton and examined the cord. "This is no problem. It is easy to fix. Tell your mother I will have it for her soon." He opened the door for them.

"Thank you," said Morton.

"Yes, thank you," Shirley said, and they hurried out the door.

They lingered in front of Otto's apartment, and soon the remote voices resumed, amid static and crackle. Shirley and Morton moved closer to the window so they could hear better.

Words—pieces of sentences floated out toward them. ". . . pouring from landing craft . . . under cover of warships . . . within shell range . . . hidden in ridges and embankments . . ."

Shirley didn't know what it all meant. But she was even more sure now that she wasn't jumping to conclusions about Otto, as her mother had suggested. After all, weren't the newspapers warning of spies? Weren't there posters all around, cautioning that THE ENEMY IS LISTENING and CARELESS TALK COSTS LIVES? One poster especially tugged at Shirley's heart. It showed a sad-eyed cocker spaniel, his head on a sailor's uniform, and above him a gold-star flag, which meant that a serviceman had been killed in the war. The poster read HE DIED BECAUSE SOMEONE TALKED.

And here was Otto with this radio. And what

did he do in the garage? He was either a spy or a saboteur or both.

After taking a Kool-Aid-ice-cube break in Morton's apartment, they drew pictures of Hitler and Hirohito on the sidewalk with chalk. Shirley took a picture of their artwork, and then, with great pleasure, they rubbed out the chalk faces with their shoes. That's when they saw Otto emerging from the garage.

He reached into his pocket for his keys and, when he pulled them out, a piece of paper fell to the ground. Shirley and Morton glanced at each other. Then they shifted their glances toward Otto, who locked the door and turned into the alley in the direction of Thirteenth Street.

Shirley and Morton ran to retrieve the paper.

"What does it say?" Shirley looked over Morton's shoulder.

"I can't read it. It's written either in code or a foreign language."

"Maybe it's German," said Shirley. "I think we should follow him. This could be the most important thing we do. Even more important than the victory garden or anything else. We could catch a spy."

They spotted Otto walking along Thirteenth Street and were behind him when he turned right on Independence Boulevard. They were behind him when he made another right on Roosevelt Road and headed toward the Road Theater.

Was Otto going to the movies? Shirley wondered. That could be a spy thing to do. Spies could watch movies to learn about the American way of life. She heard people on the radio talk about the American way of life all the time.

But Otto passed the theater without even bothering to see what was playing. Up ahead was Lubin's candy store and Ye Olde Chocolate Shoppe, where Shirley and Irv had first experienced the delight of a hot fudge sundae. Was Otto going for a hot fudge sundae? She was disappointed. That wasn't a very spy-like thing to do. And yet, she supposed that spies, too, ate hot fudge sundaes sometimes.

But Otto didn't stop for a sundae. He continued on until he came to the hardware store. He looked in the window for a moment and went inside.

"The hardware store. I should've known," said Morton. "You can get lots of sabotage stuff in a hardware store. Let's give him some time, and then we'll go in, too."

Shirley took a picture of the hardware store before they slipped quietly inside. They crept behind the counters to the school supplies and fiddled with the pencils and sharpeners while they watched Otto. He was behind some tall garden tools, but they still had a pretty good view of him.

"Look," said Shirley. "He's getting batteries . . . and tape."

"And wires. Sabotage stuff if I ever saw any."

"And matches. Holy smokes, Morton, he's going to blow up the whole place."

Otto took his supplies to the cashier and set them on the counter. They waited until he left the store and then followed him back along Roosevelt Road.

"One of these days he'll slip up," said Morton. "I once saw a movie where a German spy posed as an American soldier. But the other soldiers discovered he was a spy when he didn't know who won the 1940 World Series."

"Who *did* win the 1940 World Series?"

"I can't remember. But that guy didn't know anything about baseball. That's how they knew he wasn't an American."

Shirley remembered a movie about a spy who slipped up. The spy was an American who pretended to be German. He was very convincing until he slipped up while eating in a German restaurant. He was cutting his food with the knife in his right hand and the fork in his left. When it came time to eat, he placed the knife on the plate and switched the fork to his right hand. By this seemingly insignificant action, the American had blown his cover. It was seen by a German officer, who approached him and said, "You—American—you are under arrest." Too bad the American hadn't known that a German would not have switched his fork to the other hand.

Yes, a slip-up. That's what they needed.

They walked along Independence, noticing again the white flags with the blue stars hanging in some of the windows. In the window of a small basement apartment hung a flag with a gold star, like the one on the poster with the cocker spaniel. Shirley thought how in that very apartment people were mourning for a husband or father or brother or son. A son like Manny. Or any one of Shirley's cousins.

Shirley and Morton gazed at the flag in silent tribute. A plane flew overhead. When they turned their attention back to the boulevard, Otto was gone.

◦ *8* ◦

Shirley was looking out of her open bedroom window. Simone Schwab and Alvin were sitting in the parked car, necking. She had been watching them for about ten minutes and wished they would hurry up and finish. She wasn't sure she could last much longer. It was a very hot day, and her room was boiling. She didn't dare stick her head out of the window, in case they saw her. But she didn't want to miss anything either. So she sat there and watched and waited for them to come up for air, which they hardly ever did. She wondered how they could breathe like that. And she wondered, too, if anyone would ever kiss her that way. Morton? No, she couldn't imagine kissing Morton, even a little.

Manny? Oh, yes. Now that was a different story. She could definitely imagine kissing Manny like that. In her imagination she and Manny were

91

in the car instead of Simone and Alvin. And their arms were around each other, and they were kissing a long, slow kiss and not coming up for air. She tingled all over.

It all felt so real to Shirley. Almost as if Manny were right in the room with her. She could feel his presence. Feel his lips brush the back of her neck, sending shivers down her spine, stirring all kinds of new and unfamiliar feelings within her. She touched a hand to the back of her neck, turned suddenly, and screamed.

"Irving, you jerk! You get away from me!"

Irv threw himself onto his bed, laughing hysterically. "You—you should've seen your face just now." He rolled across the bed, then sat up, clutching his stomach, still laughing.

"You're not funny. You scared me half to death."

She was angry with him for invading her private thoughts. Embarrassed, too, until it occurred to her that there was no way he could have witnessed the scene played out in her mind.

"It serves you right for spying on them."

"I wasn't spying on anyone. I was just looking out the window."

"Sure you were."

Irv watched with her for a few minutes and

made funny little kissing sounds every once in a while. He did not take love seriously. Even when he was at the movies, he either made fun of the actors when they kissed or he booed them. And he cheered the cowboys because cowboys never kissed.

"Ah, my darling," he said in his Charles Boyer voice, "come with me to the gas pipe."

Shirley giggled at Irv's imitation of the French actor Charles Boyer saying, "Come with me to the Casbah." The Casbah was a far-off, mysterious place where romance, danger, and adventure happened. Irv liked to substitute the words *gas pipe*.

"You mean *Casbah*. Come with me to the Casbah."

"That's what I said," said Irv in his Irv voice. And then he became French again. "Come with me to the gas pipe." He kissed himself all over his hands and arms.

Shirley knew what was coming next. It was part of Irv's Charles Boyer routine. He criss-crossed his arms in front of his chest and placed a hand on each shoulder. Then he turned around, his back facing Shirley. From the back it looked as if he were being hugged. More than being hugged, he made it seem that he was engaged in a passionate embrace. Irv made more kissing sounds, followed by "Ah, my darling, let me whisper sweet nothings in your ear. Sweet nothing, sweet nothing, sweet nothing."

Shirley was laughing so hard she was sure that Simone and Alvin would hear her. She tried to get Irv to stop fooling around. But once he got going, it was hard to stop him.

"I've got to get out of here," said Shirley. She ran from the room, laughing, and went out to the back porch. Stinky was lapping up some water from her dish, and Shirley went over to pet her.

"Hot out, isn't it, Stinky? Did you know that Irving is crazy?"

Stinky looked up at Shirley for a few moments, switched her tail against Shirley's arms, tickling her, and continued drinking. Shirley fluffed up the blanket in Stinky's box to make it more comfortable for her. Then she went down to check on the victory garden.

Little green things were poking out of the dry earth. But Shirley couldn't tell the difference between the vegetables and the weeds. She went back upstairs, filled half a pail from the kitchen faucet, and watered the green things. She was just about finished pouring water from a second pailful when she heard someone calling.

"Shirley, Shirley." It was Morton calling her

from the alley. He was calling and running into the lot at the same time. And he was carrying a box.

"Shirley, look what I found in the alley."

"What's in the box, Morton?"

"Just look inside."

Shirley couldn't believe what she saw. There were cartons and cartons of Lucky Strike cigarettes. "My God, Morton, where did these come from?" Shirley knew that cigarettes were rationed and hard to get.

"I told you," said Morton, still out of breath. "I found them in the alley." Then he picked up the box and started running up the steps. "Ma, Ma, look what I found in the alley. Come out here."

"The alley?" Mrs. Kaminsky called back from her kitchen. "How many times did I tell you not to pick up things from the alley? Did you forget about the rat trap so soon?"

Mrs. Kaminsky was referring to the time Morton had come running home screaming because his finger was caught in a rat trap. He had picked it up because he thought it was a printing press.

"It's not a rat trap, Ma. It's cigarettes."

"What?" Mrs. Kaminsky screeched, running out the door with Harold. "Cigarettes?"

Not only did Mrs. Kaminsky run out to the

porch; so did Shirley's mother and Mrs. Kaluzna. Irv came pedaling into the lot on his bicycle just then, too.

"What's all the commotion about?" Mrs. Cohen asked.

"Morton found tons of cigarettes in the alley," said Shirley. "Maybe Daddy can switch to Luckies."

"Wow, black-market cigarettes," said Irv.

"You shouldn't touch," said Mrs. Kaluzna. "Maybe they're poisoned."

Shirley ran in to get her Brownie.

"I've got to get a picture of all these cigarettes," she said as she came out again. "No one would believe it." She took aim and snapped a picture.

"Tell me again," said Mrs. Kaminsky. "Exactly where did you find these?"

"All the way down at the end of the alley," said Morton, pointing. "Where I fell on the glass that time and cut my wrist."

"Show me. And take the box with you."

Morton led the way to the alley, followed by Shirley, Stinky, Mrs. Kaminsky carrying Harold, and Irv on his bike. Mrs. Kaluzna called after them, "Save me a few packs."

At the end of the alley Morton stopped in front

of a garage with its door open. "In there," he said. "On the floor."

"This is where you found them?" asked Mrs. Kaminsky. "You said the alley."

"Yeah. Part of the box was sticking out into the alley."

"Put them back."

"Aw, Ma."

"I said put them back and let's go."

"And fast," said Irv. "We'd better not get mixed up with any black-market gangsters."

Morton put the box back in the garage and kicked at an old tire on his way out.

"Don't feel so bad," Shirley said. "They were only cigarettes. It would've been different if you found a box of Dubble Bubble."

"Yeah. I don't care. Anyway, my father smokes cigars."

"Let's go find Howie," said Shirley, trying to take Morton's mind off the cigarettes. Irv rode away on his bike while Mrs. Kaminsky mumbled something about going on a wild goose chase and missing the latest episode of "Backstage Wife."

Shirley and Morton crossed the alley to Howie's backyard. Morton cupped his hands around his mouth and called up to the third floor.

"Yo, Howieeee."

After a few moments, Howie appeared on his back porch.

"Whatcha doin'?" Morton called up to him.

"Listening to the ball game. The Cubs are winning one to nothing. Nicholson just hit a homer."

Shirley was happy to hear that. The Chicago Cubs were her favorite team, and Bill Nicholson was her favorite player.

"You coming down or you gonna stay and listen to the game?" Morton asked.

"It's too hot inside. I'll be right down."

"Someday we'll be able to see the game on television," said Morton while they were waiting.

"Television?" Shirley asked. The word was only vaguely familiar.

"Yeah. They're inventing something called television. It's like radio, only you can see the programs."

"You can see the programs? You mean you can see the people and everything?"

"Sure."

"I don't believe it."

"It's true. Just ask Howie."

"I will," said Shirley.

"Howie, are they really inventing television, where you can see the programs?" she asked as soon as he came down to the yard.

"They've already invented it. But it's not

around much—because of the war. Probably after the war everybody will be able to get a set."

"See, I told you," said Morton.

"Wow," said Shirley. And she imagined watching the Cubs right in her own dining room. Or watching "Captain Midnight" and "The Lone Ranger." All her favorite programs. It was too good to believe.

"Hey," said Howie. "I've got fifteen cents on me. My ma let me keep the money I got from returning the pop bottles. Anyone want some ice cream?"

"Oh boy," said Shirley. "We can get Dixies." And better than that, she would get to see Manny.

They walked back through the alley toward Douglas Boulevard. And when they reached the garage with the open door, Morton showed Howie where he found the cigarettes.

"That's the box. Want us to show you how many cartons there are inside?"

"Let's not," said Shirley. "Irv says they're black market."

Shirley didn't even know what Irv meant by black market, but she wasn't taking any chances. She wondered if bubble gum could be black market.

"Howie," she asked. "Could there be such a thing as black-market bubble gum?"

"Sure. Let's say someone gets an illegal supply of bubble gum somewhere. And bubble gum ordinarily costs a penny apiece. But there's a shortage now, and people can't get any except from this person. So he can charge whatever he wants. Fifty cents, or even a dollar apiece. And if people are desperate enough for bubble gum, they'll pay it."

"I'm desperate enough," said Shirley. "But I couldn't afford to pay more than a nickel apiece." She thought of Felicia Lieberman and wondered if she had black-market bubble gum.

"So this guy with the cigarettes. Is he buying or selling?" Morton asked.

"Either one," said Howie. "Maybe he belongs to a whole gang of guys who bought up tons of cigarettes from all around the country, and now they're selling each pack for some fantastic price and are making a million bucks."

"The crooks," said Shirley. "Let's go get the Dixies before somebody invents black-market ice cream."

In the drugstore, Morton and Howie went over to look at the comic books while Shirley went to look for Manny. She found him stacking first aid kits on a shelf. Shirley tucked herself in and smoothed wisps of hair behind her ears. She checked her laces to make sure they were tied. Then she concentrated on Manny.

She watched him stoop to pick up more kits from the floor, watched him arrange them on the shelf and stoop down again. He was wearing his white apron, and the belt was coming untied. She longed to move close to him and tie it for him and circle her arms around his waist.

She really didn't want him to leave. Having him here would be better than writing letters. Better than being his girl back home. She wanted to be *his girl*—now!

It was almost as if Manny could sense that Shirley was watching him. He turned around.

"Hey, Shirl. It's good to see you. Can I interest you in a first aid kit?"

"I don't think so. We've got plenty at home."

"You used to be one of our best customers. I remember your mother always coming in at the beginning of summer to stock up on bandages and Mercurochrome. You were forever needing to be patched up. Your knees and elbows, mostly."

"I guess I don't fall so much anymore."

"Well, you look pretty much in one piece to me."

They started walking toward the door, where Morton and Howie were still looking through the comic books.

"When are you leaving?" Shirley asked.

"In a few days."

"So soon?"

"Yep. And I sure will miss you guys." He smiled at her.

Shirley lowered her eyes and stared at her shoes. "We'll miss you, too, Manny."

"He'll be back before you know it."

She looked up to see Mr. Zelnick standing with his arm around Manny. They looked so happy together, and yet there was such a sadness in Mr. Zelnick's eyes. Shirley would miss Manny terribly, but she knew she couldn't even begin to imagine how hard it was for Mr. Zelnick to send his only son off to war. It was impossible to imagine Irv going away to fight.

Shirley knew she would never forget this scene. And it was one that she wanted to capture on film. "Hold it just like that," she told Manny and his father. And there, near the open door, with the sunlight streaming in, Shirley snapped a picture of Mr. Zelnick and Manny with their arms around each other. Morton and Howie stood next to her as she took it.

"You'll treat my friends real good while I'm away, won't you, Pop?"

"I'll take good care of them. Don't you worry." He patted Manny's shoulder and quietly walked away. Manny's eyes followed him for a few moments.

"If you guys can come in every once in a while and sort of keep an eye on him, I'd appreciate it," Manny said. "He likes kids."

"Sure we will," said Shirley. "And if you want, I can write to you and let you know how things are around here. Or if you ever just feel like writing . . . I'd answer."

"Me and Howie will write to you, too," Morton said quickly.

Clod! Shirley wanted to call him. She thought it was the right word to describe Morton right now, for interrupting. She had once heard it used in a movie. A woman had called some guy a clod because she was hopelessly in love with him, and he was too insensitive to realize it. Morton, of course, had no idea how Shirley felt about Manny, but he had no business butting in. The clod!

"Sounds good," said Manny. "We've got your addresses on file here. I might just take them with me." He placed his hands on his hips. "Now—is there something you guys wanted?"

"Yeah," said Howie. "Three Dixies. Chocolate."

Manny took out three Dixie cups from the freezer and handed one to each of them, along with a flat wooden spoon.

Howie took fifteen cents out of his pocket.

"Forget it," said Manny. "It's my treat." He

held out his hand to Morton and Howie. "In case I
don't see you again before I go . . ." He shook
hands with each of them. Then he clasped Shirley's hand in both of his, winked at her, and
curled her fingers over something that he placed
in her palm.

Shirley uncurled her fingers as they walked
out of the store. There in her hand was a piece of
Dubble Bubble. It was so like Manny to do something like that. She carefully placed it in her
pocket, while Morton and Howie were already lift-
ing the lids of their Dixie cups to see which movie
star's face appeared on the other side.

"Roy Rogers, king of the cowboys," Morton
announced.

"Nuts," said Howie. "Dorothy Lamour. What
do I want with Dorothy Lamour? You want it,
Shirley?"

"Huh? Oh, no, thanks. I already have about
five Dorothy Lamours in my collection." Shirley
couldn't think of movie stars right now. All she
could think about was Manny, and the way he
had clasped her hand in his and winked at her.
And that he was leaving, and she didn't know if
she would ever see him again.

They crossed Independence Boulevard to the
park and sat under a tree to eat their ice cream,
which by this time was melting around the edges.

Morton and Howie were discussing the black market while Shirley was trying to decide if she should save the gum or chew it. She knew she had to give it lots of thought. She was in a hurry to get home.

"Let's go," said Shirley, dumping the empty Dixie cup into a trash can. "I'll race you guys to the end of the park."

Morton and Howie dumped their Dixies, too.

"Okay," said Morton, using his foot to draw a line in the ground for all of them to stand behind. "On your mark, get set, go!"

They were off! They ran across the park, with Shirley taking the lead almost immediately. At first she imagined herself racing, not with Morton or Howie, but with the cars and buses along the boulevard. But then there was only Shirley, flying like the wind. She could barely feel her blouse inching out of her shorts, her shoelaces becoming untied, and her already loose braids loosening more. There was only Shirley Frances Cohen, with her skinny legs, strong and sure, carrying her to victory.

° **9** °

To chew or not to chew. That was the question Shirley asked herself after the race home. She sat at the edge of her bed, trying to reach a decision.

She turned the gum over and over in her fingers, feeling its thick, round shape, and lifted it to her nose so she could breathe in that wonderful, familiar Dubble Bubble smell.

Of course she should chew it. What was the good of having a piece of bubble gum if she couldn't enjoy it? Unless it was to save. To smell and look at whenever she wanted to. To keep for always because Manny had given it to her. But Manny gave it to her to chew. It was a hard decision.

Slowly she undid the twisted ends of the wrapper and removed the small pink chunk. She brought it up to her mouth, hesitated for a moment, then sank her teeth into it and bit off half.

It was a little hard at first, but it softened quickly, and the sweet juices began to flow. It was pure heaven. When the gum was soft enough, she pushed her tongue through it and blew. The most beautiful bubble began to grow in front of her. It was a pretty large one, too. Imagine if she had used the whole piece of gum.

As she chewed and blew, she wrapped up the rest of the piece and stuck it in her drawer to save for another time. She didn't know when.

Every morning after breakfast, Shirley treated herself to a whiff of bubble gum from the piece she had put away and checked the mail for her shuffleboard set. She really didn't expect to find it so soon. It always seemed like a year before she received the things she sent away for. But she was hoping.

Nothing was waiting for her in the hallway when she checked one morning, and there were just two lonely pieces of mail in the mailbox. She touched her finger to the small, round hole in the glass pane of the hallway door. "This was made by someone with a BB gun," Irv had once told her. More than anything, Irv wanted a BB gun. But when he finally received one as a Bar Mitzvah present from their Uncle Jack, Mrs. Cohen made him exchange it for a pair of hockey skates.

When Shirley took the mail up to the apartment, she found her mother standing in front of the dining room mirror, pinning up her hair. "Anybody want to come shopping with me?" she asked, taking a hairpin out of her mouth. "We'll take the streetcar over to Homan Avenue."

"I throw up on the streetcar," said Shirley.

"You throw up on anything that moves," Irv told her.

Mrs. Cohen gave herself a final check in the mirror. "I thought we'd take a ride to Sears."

"Sears?" Irv shrieked. "No, no, anything but that!" He grasped his throat, slithered to the floor, and lay there, gasping.

"Too bad you're busy dying and can't go with her," Shirley said. "Maybe you could steer Ma to the BB guns and convince her to buy you one."

Irv stopped gasping and sat up. "Hey, Ma. Think it would work?"

"Sure, sure," said Mrs. Cohen, checking the amount of money she had in her coin purse. "I'll buy you a BB gun the day man goes to the moon."

Irv fell back onto the floor, and Shirley went out to the porch with her camera and a glass of milk for Stinky. The cat wasn't around. Shirley could hear Morton and Marilyn in the victory garden. Maybe Stinky was with them. She poured the milk into the cat's dish and ran down to the garden. Morton and Marilyn were bending over the plants. Shirley's eyes searched the garden for Stinky, but she wasn't there.

"Did either of you guys see Stinky?"

"Not yet," said Morton. "But you know how she is. She likes to roam the neighborhood in the morning when it's cool."

Shirley nodded. "She'll probably come back when she's hungry. Were you pulling weeds just now?"

"Yeah," said Morton. "I think I've got it figured out."

"He had to kill a couple of radishes first," said Marilyn, holding out the plants to Shirley.

Shirley had never seen such tiny radishes. "Oh, they're adorable," she said. "But it's so sad. They'll never grow up."

"I pulled them out by mistake," Morton apologized. "But now we'll know how to recognize the radishes. By their leaves. And we'll know which ones the watermelons are. Everything else will be either carrots or weeds. And we'll figure it out eventually."

"How do we recognize the watermelons?" Shirley asked.

"Just compare it to my special watermelon plant."

There in the corner was Morton's tiny watermelon plant, somewhat shriveled. Shirley suspected that he had watered it in his special way many times since that first time. She snapped a picture of the plant.

"Why is the watermelon plant special?" Marilyn asked.

"He watered it a special way," Shirley said and covered her mouth to hold in a giggle.

"But how did you water it your special way, Morton?"

"It's a complicated experiment. Too hard to explain."

They pulled out weeds and straightened up the Popsicle-stick markers, though the packets were worn and ragged now, having been rained on and torn by the wind. But the garden looked neat and clean. And it was easier to recognize the vegetable plants.

As they were admiring their garden, familiar voices echoed across the lot. They turned to see Howie and Donnie running toward them.

"Guess what?" shouted Donnie. "We're having a blackout tonight."

"Really?" asked Shirley. "How do you know?" Shirley loved blackouts—when everyone turned off all their lights so if enemy planes flew over, which they never did, the pilots wouldn't be able to see where to drop their bombs. Blackouts were very exciting, with the sirens sounding and every-one except the air-raid wardens having to take cover indoors.

"He heard the big shots talking," said Howie.

Donnie lived in the same building as the pre-cinct captain, the alderman, and the sheriff of Cook County.

"Finally we get to do something really impor-tant," said Shirley.

The Victory Club had decided at an earlier meeting that for the next blackout, instead of run-ning home and hiding under their tables, they would be junior air-raid wardens and stay outside to spot enemy planes.

"Let's each make armbands," said Shirley. "That way we'll be identified as junior air-raid wardens, and no one will chase us inside. And we'll make something for Stinky to wear. Maybe a sign that says JUNIOR AIR-RAID CAT." She glanced around the lot. "Where is that cat already? She should have been back by now. Unless . . ." She turned to Morton. "Do you think . . . maybe . . ."

"The buggy!" said Morton, and he turned and ran down the steps to the basement, with every-one following. He turned on the light, hurried over to the buggy, and made his second important announcement as president.

"She had her babies!"

"Oh, Stinky," Shirley cried out. "You did it!"

Everyone crowded around the buggy and saw Stinky licking her nursing kittens. Shirley longed to touch them. But then the other kids would pet them, too. And that might disturb the kittens or worry Stinky.

"Move back a little," said Shirley, waving them away. "Give her room to breathe."

"Ooh, they're so tiny," Marilyn squealed. "How many are there?"

"Four, I think," said Shirley. "No—five. There's a little gray one hidden over here."

They counted the kittens. Two gray, two black, and one striped alley cat, just like Stinky. Shirley figured that the father was probably the black cat she had seen darting across the lot the other day.

"I wish I could take their picture," said Shirley. "But it's too dark down here, and the flash might scare them." She petted Stinky, who closed her eyes, the little motor running inside her. She spoke softly to her. "Congratulations, sweetie. You're a mommy now."

Stinky opened her eyes, looked up at Shirley, and yawned.

"I think we should let her rest," said Shirley. "And now that she's a brand-new mother, we can forget about that sign." She found a cover from a mason jar, rinsed and filled it from the faucet in the laundry tub, and held it out to Stinky. Shirley watched with pleasure as the cat lapped it up thirstily. "We'll come back in a little while and bring her something to eat." She petted Stinky one more time before they left.

After everyone had gone home for lunch, she returned with a dish of cottage cheese for Stinky. While Stinky ate, Shirley stroked the tiny kitten heads and laughed at the way they crawled around, moving their front legs forward and dragging their hind legs along. She was glad for the chance to be alone with them. To have them all to herself.

Shirley was so excited about the kittens—and the blackout—she could hardly eat supper that evening.

"Five kittens," she said, as she passed her father the corn on the cob. "One kitten for each member of the Victory Club."

"It sounds like five too many kittens for Thirteenth Street," said her mother.

"Don't worry. None of the others can keep any. Their mothers aren't as nice as you."

"Thank you for the compliment. But we can't keep any either."

"Aw, Ma, come on. Just one little kitten. You should see how cute they are. I've got my eye on the striped one. She's a carbon copy of Stinky."

113

"I've seen them. And they're very cute. But they grow up to become cats. And we already have Stinky."

"But Stinky is an outdoor cat. That doesn't count."

"And what happens in the winter, when it gets freezing cold outside? We'll have to take her in."

"You mean it? We can keep her in the house?" Shirley had been wondering what she and Morton would do with Stinky in the winter, but she hadn't wanted to bring up the subject with her parents before it was necessary.

Mrs. Cohen shrugged. "What else can we do? We can't let her freeze."

"But who can we give the kittens to? I don't know anybody who can keep any."

"Maybe I can take one for the factory," said Shirley's father. "We've got mice."

"Take two. So they'll have company."

A tapping on the screen door interrupted any further discussion about kittens.

"Your boyfriend is here," Shirley's father whispered to her mother.

Shirley looked up to see a man with a smiling face, tipping his cap. It was the banana man.

"Harry, stop it," said Mrs. Cohen with a wave of a hand, pretending she didn't enjoy the joke. "Come right in," she called to the peddler.

They all liked to kid Mrs. Cohen about how the banana man was in love with her. After all, only the banana man made house calls, and only to Mrs. Cohen. He always brought her his best bananas. At all other times, he joined the rest of the peddlers—the watermelon man and the vegetable man—in the alley. They parked their horse-drawn wagons there and waited for the neighborhood women to come by and do their shopping.

The banana man walked into the kitchen, tipped his cap again, and smiled at Mrs. Cohen. "I brought you the best. And I give you a good price."

Shirley and Irv sat at the table, snickering. Then Irv began humming "Besame Mucho," a love song that he enjoyed making fun of. Sometimes, instead of singing "besame mucho," he substituted the words *besame pee you-cho.*

"Have a seat," said Mr. Cohen, "and I'll get you something to drink." Shirley's father poured the banana man a small glass of sweet red wine, and while he sat sipping, Mrs. Cohen selected the bananas she wanted.

The banana man, Shirley noted, spoke with an accent. It wasn't a Yiddish accent, she knew, and since he didn't sound like the Nazis in the movies, she decided it wasn't German either.

"What kind of accent does the banana man have?" Shirley asked when he left.

"Greek, I think," said her mother.

"Good," said Shirley. "At least I don't have to worry about him being a spy."

"I don't think you have to worry about spies," her father said. "I doubt if we have any around here. All we have are Democrats."

"What about Otto?"

"Otto again," said her mother. "Shirley, please. What has he ever done to you? Let the man alone. I'm sure he's had his share of trouble."

"What kind of trouble?"

Mrs. Cohen shrugged.

"Then how do you know he's had trouble?"

"By his eyes. Sometimes you can read a person's trouble in his eyes. I want you to stop this spy talk. It's dangerous talk."

"Then how do you explain the stuff he's doing in the garage and the shortwave radio Morton and I saw in his apartment?"

"How do you know it's shortwave?" Irv asked.

"Morton said so."

"Morton? The same Morton who thought a rat trap was a printing press?"

"How was he supposed to know what it was?

116

He never saw a rat trap before." She buttered some corn and sprinkled salt on it. Irv took it from her.

"For me? Thanks." He gave her another one.

"Did you hear Otto send any messages?" Mr. Cohen asked.

"Well, no. But that doesn't mean he doesn't send them at other times."

"Maybe he just likes to listen to broadcasts from England. Lots of people do."

"Maybe," said Shirley. "And maybe not." She buttered and salted the second cob and began eating. "We're having a blackout tonight."

"How would you know?" asked Irv.

"The Victory Club knows about these things."

After supper, Shirley, Morton, and Marilyn— all wearing armbands decorated with stars and stripes and announcing that they were junior air-raid wardens—went into the basement to take another look at the kittens. All five were nursing on Stinky, who looked up at her visitors with half-closed eyes. But she opened them wide when she smelled the plate of sardines that Morton had brought her. When the kids came out, they found Howie and Donnie waiting for them on the steps.

Donnie was wearing his sergeant shirt, and

they were both wearing their armbands. But what caught Shirley's eye were the badges. Badges with photos of President Roosevelt on them. They were both wearing them on their shirts.

"Roosevelt badges!" Shirley cried out. "Where did you get them?"

"From the alderman," Donnie said, spilling buttons and badges out of a bag onto one of the steps. "See, all sizes. Aren't they keen? Take your pick."

Shirley picked out one of each kind and pinned them on her polo shirt. Morton and Marilyn each took a few, too. The buttons and badges were more than Shirley had ever hoped for. She ran into the house to show them to her mother and father and to Irv. Then she came back out with her mother and her camera so that Mrs. Cohen could record the event.

"You all look very patriotic," Mrs. Cohen said as she snapped their picture and wound the film. "We're lucky to have gotten this shot. It's the last one."

"See," said Shirley, when they set out to take the film to Zelnick's. "These badges show how good President Roosevelt is. Why else would they make badges of him?"

"They have badges of Dewey, too," said Howie.

"They do?"

"Sure. Once I saw somebody wearing one."

Shirley couldn't ever imagine anybody wanting to wear a Dewey badge, or wanting to be a Republican, for that matter. She didn't even know any Republicans. Just like she didn't know any White Sox fans. Everyone she knew was a Democrat and a Cubs fan.

When they returned from the drugstore, they sat on the steps watching fireflies and waiting for the air-raid drill and night to come. As darkness approached, it happened. The sirens blasted. Morton gave the command, "Let's go!" And the junior air-raid wardens mobilized.

Morton pulled the goggles over his eyes and scanned the skies, while Shirley immediately began looking around for some little kids to chase home. When she couldn't find any, she just walked around the lot, feeling important and proud, with her armband and badges. President Roosevelt would be proud, too, if he only knew what she and the Victory Club were doing on the home front.

Irv dashed into the lot with some drawings of Hitler, Mussolini, and Hirohito and spread them out on the ground.

"Don't anyone step on these," he called to

the others. "I want them to be in good shape in case any bombs fall." Then he ran back into the apartment.

Except for the Victory Club and the fireflies darting about, the lot was empty. So were the porches. From where Shirley could see, no one was walking along the boulevard either. Everyone, it seemed, had gone inside to seek shelter. Everyone but the junior air-raid wardens. And one other person.

"Holy smokes," said Donnie. "He's at it again."

"At what? Who?" asked the junior air-raid wardens. And then they saw him, too. Otto, emerging from the garage, carrying the black box and a shopping bag.

"What does he do in there?" Shirley whispered.

"Maybe it's got something to do with the blackout," said Morton.

"Look," said Howie. "He forgot to lock the door. We've got to get a look in there when the coast is clear."

Otto started toward the basement but stopped when he saw them. "What are you doing here?" he demanded. "You should not be outside. Go home."

When no one answered him, he continued down the basement steps.

"He just doesn't want us to spot the enemy planes," said Shirley when Otto was out of earshot.

"Well, we're not listening to him," said Morton. "We're staying out here, no matter what. Nothing's going to stop us from spotting enemy planes."

Then, from Morton's porch came a voice, hollering, "Morton Kaminsky, you get inside here this minute."

"Aw, Ma."

"Don't 'aw, Ma' me. Just get in here. And Marilyn, you, too."

From across the alley, Mrs. Jacobs came after Howie, and then Shirley's mother was out on the porch.

"Shirley, the sirens. Didn't you hear the sirens? Come inside."

"But Ma . . ."

"No *buts*. Come in right now."

"I'd better get going before they come after me, too," said Donnie, and he ran off.

Shirley stomped past her mother. "This is no way to win a war." She went inside and joined Irv under the kitchen table, while her mother and father went around the apartment making sure that all the window shades were down and the lights were off.

"What can we do now?" Shirley asked.

"Just wait for the planes to come and the bombs to fall," said Irv. Shirley couldn't tell if he was joking or if he was serious.

"They wouldn't really fall here," said Shirley. "Not in America." Bombs—real bombs falling out of real enemy planes. The possibility of this actually happening frightened her.

"It can happen," said Irv.

Shirley wouldn't let herself believe that bad things could happen in America. It was just like the time Irv had told her about guns a few years ago.

They had been listening to "Gangbusters" on the radio. The people in the story were shooting each other all over the place, and it scared Shirley. "I'm glad there's no such thing as guns," she had said.

"Sure there are," Irv had answered her.

"But not in America."

"In America, too."

Guns in America? Killing in America? Never had Shirley been so disillusioned. She had always believed in the goodness of America. How could anything bad happen in the land of Washington, Lincoln, and the Statue of Liberty?

Now, underneath the kitchen table, Irv thrust a deck of cards into Shirley's hand. "Here, pick a card, any card."

"I can't see what the cards are in the dark."

"It doesn't matter. Just pick one."

Shirley picked a card and gave it to him.

"Thanks," said Irv, putting the card back in the deck and the deck into his pocket.

"What's the trick?" Shirley asked.

"I didn't say there was a trick. I just said to pick a card."

"You're crazy," said Shirley as she moved closer to him and waited for the all-clear signal to sound.

◦ *10* ◦

Shirley awoke to a wonderful morning. No bombs had fallen during the night, and Mr. Cohen had agreed to take two of the kittens for his factory. He even offered to make a special mattress for them to sleep on.

Irv had gone off early to help a friend catch butterflies for his collection, which meant that Shirley could get dressed in the bedroom instead of the bathroom, for once. Afterward she went into the kitchen and helped herself to some orange juice. Then she poured some milk into a bowl of Cheerioats and sliced some bananas on top of it. While she ate, she studied the Capitol Milk lid. The state, Minnesota. The capital, St. Paul. That was a good one. Shirley had lots of relatives—on her father's side—in St. Paul. She had lots of them on her mother's side in Minneapolis, too.

While she was eating, Morton came to the

door. He was holding a dish. "Are you coming out? I've got scrambled eggs for Stinky."

"In a minute." She gobbled up the rest of her cereal and poured some milk into a bowl. "Okay, let's go. I can't wait to see the kittens."

The door to the basement was open. And wafting out of the basement was the smell of freshly laundered wash. In the semidarkness Shirley heard a faint meowing. She answered it as Morton searched for the light-bulb chain.

"Don't worry, Stinky. We didn't forget about you."

Morton turned on the light, and Shirley called, "Come on out and have some breakfast. We'll watch your babies for you." Stinky just meowed and stayed where she was.

Shirley and Morton placed the dishes on the floor, and Shirley turned back to the buggy.

"Okay, now, let's see how big they—oh, my God!" Shirley clapped her hand against her mouth.

"What's wrong?" asked Morton, peering into the buggy. He let out a gasp.

Shirley stood horrified. The kittens lay strewn about the mattress, twisted and still. Tufts of fur seemed to be scattered everywhere. A thin trail of blood led from the gray-striped kitten to the edge of the mattress.

She shut her eyes and turned away. Then, gagging, she ran out of the basement. Morton ran out after her. At the top of the basement steps, she stopped to take in deep breaths of air. Then she raced up to her apartment.

She flew into the kitchen. "Ma!—Ma!" she burst out. "Where are you?"

Mrs. Cohen emerged from the dining room, holding Shirley's blue velvet dress. "Shirley, what's the matter?"

"They're dead, Ma. The kittens are dead."

Shirley felt tears begin to well up as she tried to describe what she had just seen. "They're lying crooked, and there's blood, and Stinky's just sitting there, all alone, meowing. . . ." The tears spilled out of her eyes, and she couldn't stop them. "And Stinky knows. I can tell she knows there's something wrong with her babies."

"Oh, the poor thing," said her mother, holding the blue velvet against her chest. She placed the dress on the table and headed for the door. Shirley followed her down the steps. Morton, who was sitting on the bottom step, got up to make way for them, and all three went down to the basement. Shirley couldn't bring herself to look at the kittens again. She and Morton waited outside the door while Mrs. Cohen went inside.

They watched as she cautiously approached the buggy, looked inside, and turned quickly away. Though they couldn't hear the words, they heard her speaking to the cat in a voice that was soft and low and soothing.

Through her own blurry eyes, Shirley could see Morton swipe at a tear. Soon a whole stream of tears was rolling down his cheeks, his face becoming smudged as he wiped them with his hand.

This was a side of Morton that she had never seen. Sure, she had seen him cry before. Twice. Once when he fell on that glass and cut his wrist, and the time he caught his finger in the rat trap. But those two times he was crying and screaming because he was frightened and in pain. Never before had he cried like this, softly to himself, in front of Shirley, simply because he was touched by something deeply. Even at the movies, watching *Lassie Come Home,* Shirley's face was in a perpetual state of wetness while Morton shifted around in his seat, coughed, and yawned. Anything to draw attention away from the tears that might be spilling out of his eyes, to cover up any real feelings he might have inside.

Mrs. Cohen came out of the basement shaking her head. "It's terrible. And so sad."

"How's Stinky?" Shirley asked.

"I tried to coax her out of the buggy, but she didn't want to leave. She'll come out when she's ready."

"What do you think happened to them?"

"Some animal. Another cat, maybe. Who knows?"

"It must have been so frightening for her. I wish we could've been there to save them."

They went back up the basement steps, and Mrs. Cohen continued on up to Shirley's apartment. Shirley and Morton sat on their stairway.

"What do *you* think happened?" Shirley asked.

Morton shrugged. "I don't know. Something— or someone—got to them."

"But who would want to hurt innocent little kittens?"

Morton shook his head, and for a while they sat there, neither of them speaking.

"You know we'll have to bury them," said Morton after a while.

Shirley nodded. "But later—after Stinky leaves the basement. We can't take her babies away while she's still in the buggy with them."

They went into the victory garden and passed the time weeding and watering and paying their last respects to Morton's special watermelon plant, dried up and shriveled.

"So much for experiments," said Shirley.

"The other watermelons aren't doing so good either."

"Yeah. Maybe watermelons can't grow in Chicago."

Stinky appeared in the garden and brushed up against Shirley's leg.

Shirley reached over and lifted her to her chest. "Poor baby." She held her close and stroked her fur. "I know you did what you could to protect them."

In the late hours of the afternoon, they buried the kittens at the side of the garage in a box that had once held Fanny Farmer chocolates. Shirley's mother lined the box with a piece of the casket material Mr. Cohen had brought home and placed the kittens inside. It was a comfort to Shirley, knowing that the kittens had such a lovely box to lie in.

Morton took Otto's shovel from the basement and dug the small grave while Shirley held Stinky in her arms. Once again Shirley noticed the rings of dirt and sweat around Morton's neck. Well, if he was going into pharmacy, he'd better get used to all this digging.

Morton lowered the box into the ground and began shoveling dirt over it. Shirley sprinkled a handful of dirt over it, too. She paused to remember the tiny kittens, who would never get a chance to chase mice or sleep on small mattresses made especially for them. Oh, how she wished she had taken a picture of them.

The sound of metal scraping broke the mood. Shirley and Morton looked in the direction of the alley and saw Otto moving the trash cans around. He was whistling. How could he be whistling when five kittens were lying dead in the ground?

She held Stinky closer to her chest. "Don't worry, Stinky. Things will get better. Everything will be okay."

· *11* ·

The news was all over the neighborhood. It reached the apartment on Thirteenth Street. Manny Zelnick was dead.

"He's not dead!" Shirley shouted at her mother. "It's not true."

"I'm afraid it is," said Mrs. Cohen, setting her packages on the kitchen table. "I just found out. That's all people are talking about. In the grocery, on the streets." She wiped her forehead with a handkerchief and sat down at the table, where Shirley had been building a model airplane out of balsa wood.

"It's not exactly clear what happened. They think it has something to do with the shots they gave him."

Shirley shook her head and waved her mother away. "They made a mistake. They don't know what they're talking about."

Mrs. Cohen drew her chair closer. "Shirley, I understand how bad you must feel. This is the first time someone you know has died. Someone young and . . ."

Shirley didn't want to listen to any more. She ran to her room and threw herself onto her bed, sobbing and getting the chenille bedspread damp with tears.

Her mother didn't understand. No one did. How could anyone understand how special he was to her? And she was special to him. Even though he might not have known it yet.

It wasn't possible. Not too long ago, she had seen him. Spoken to him. Touched his hand. How could he be dead? She let loose a whole new wave of tears.

When there were no tears left, Shirley lay quietly on the bed, plucking at the yarn on the bedspread. She would miss him so much. She would've been his girl. They would've written letters. They would've hugged and kissed in a parked car. And now none of that would ever happen. She'd never see him again. Never. No matter how long Shirley lived—even if she lived to be a hundred, she would never see Manny again.

Shirley sat up in panic. Even now, in her mind, she couldn't see him! She had forgotten what he looked like. She rushed to her dresser and searched through the pictures in her drawer. There had to be a picture of Manny somewhere. She must have taken one of him. She searched all over. But there were none. And then she remembered—the roll of film she had taken in for developing the night of the blackout. Maybe there was a picture of him on that one—if it came out all right. All she found now was the small piece of Dubble Bubble, still in its wrapper. She took it out of the drawer and placed it in her other hand, curling her fingers over it the way Manny had done. She tried to picture his smile, his wink. But she couldn't. She went out to the porch.

The Victory Club was sitting on the steps.

"Hi, Shirley. Did you hear?" asked Morton.

Shirley nodded and sat down.

"I heard it was from a dirty needle," said Howie. "From the shots they gave him. He must have gotten blood poisoning."

"My mother heard he was allergic," said Marilyn.

Donnie picked at his sergeant stripes. "It's not fair. He never even got to go overseas. He didn't even get a chance to fight."

"It never would've happened if it wasn't for those lousy Germans and Japs," Morton said.

"I wonder if it hurt him when he died," Shirley said softly. She wondered what it was like for him, those last moments. Was somebody with him? A doctor? A nurse holding his hand? Or was he all alone? She couldn't bear to think that he was alone. She pushed the thought out of her mind.

She spotted the Atlas Mattress truck parked across the lot near the alley. She got up and walked slowly toward it, kicking stones along the way and hoping nobody would follow her.

She climbed up into the truck and sat behind the steering wheel. Usually it was fun to pretend she was driving. She'd turn the wheel around and make driving sounds, "Vroom, vroom." But today she just crossed her arms on the wheel and pressed her face against them.

Shirley remembered how in spring, she and Morton had been trying to fly their kites on Douglas Boulevard. They couldn't even get them off the ground. Manny had come out of the drugstore to show them how to get the kites up in the air and keep them afloat.

She thought about the time he had delivered a prescription to her house when she was sick. He had poked his head into her room and made a face, getting her to laugh for the first time that day.

The drugstore would never be the same

without Manny. "Two chocolate malteds coming up . . . I'll make them extra thick for you . . . don't tell the boss." Poor Mr. Zelnick. And Mrs. Zelnick. How awful it had to be for them.

Shirley reminded herself about the gum, still in her hand, and straightened up. She held it to her nose, closed her eyes, and breathed in the sweet bubble gum smell. Manny's face came into focus now. He was smiling at Shirley as he placed the gum in her hand. He knew how much she had wanted it. And he wanted her to have it.

Shirley unwrapped the rest of the Fleer and slowly licked off the powdery sugar before sinking her teeth into the gum, softening it and savoring the special Dubble Bubble flavor that filled her mouth. As she chewed, she carefully folded the wrapper and placed it in her pocket. She sat in the truck, chewing and blowing bubbles. A single, slow tear trickled down her cheek to the side of her mouth. She wiped it with her tongue and let it mingle with the taste of the gum.

"Hey, Shirley." Irv was standing at the open window of the truck.

Quickly Shirley wiped her eyes before the next tears had a chance to escape. She looked at Irv.

"We're getting a game going, and we can use another player."

Shirley glanced out into the lot and saw some of Irv's friends tossing a baseball around. The club members were gone. She glanced back at him.

"So—do you want to play?"

Was she hearing right? How many times had she asked him—pleaded with him—to let her play, and he had ignored her? Now of all times.

"Well?"

Shirley shook her head. "No, thanks. Not today."

Irv opened the door of the truck. "We can really use you to even up the sides."

Shirley hesitated.

"Come on. You'll hit one for Manny."

Shirley smiled up at Irv. Then she climbed out of the truck.

"Okay," Irv called out. "We've got our man. Let's choose up sides."

"That's no man," Arthur Pelton called back. "That's Polly Pigtails." The other boys laughed along with him.

"Cut it out, guys," said Irv. "She can run the bases faster than any of you. And probably hit better, too." He handed Shirley the bat.

Shirley felt a surge of love for her brother. It was wonderful the way he always stuck up for her. He teased her whenever he felt like it. But he never let anyone else do it.

"Then you can have her," said Arthur. "And to show you how fair I am, you can have Ivan, too."

"Okay by me," said Ivan. Ivan was a big guy who was a powerful hitter, but slow on his feet.

They finished choosing sides and decided that Irv's team would be up to bat first. Shirley would be number one in the lineup.

They probably just wanted to get rid of her, Shirley figured, as she took her stance at home plate. Strike out the little girl and then play some real ball. Well, she would show them. She'd hit that ball clear across the lot to Independence Boulevard.

Shirley took a few practice swings before Arthur wound up and pitched the first ball. It was high, but she swung at it anyway. She missed.

Laughter came from the outfield. "Ignore them," Irv advised. "And don't swing unless it's good."

Shirley readied herself for the second pitch. She would hit that next ball. She was sure of it. The ball came at her. She imagined it to be Hitler and Otto all rolled into one. She swung with all her might. The bat and ball connected. Shirley dropped the bat and ran.

To the cheers of her teammates, Shirley sped toward first base, running as fast as she could.

Faster than in her races with Morton and Howie. Faster even than in her race with Irv around the Douglas Park Lagoon. She was running for Manny, who would never run again. She was lightning as she hit second base; she was Superman as she sped to third, and, like Superman, she would fly in for the finish.

And fly in she did. But the sky and the ground played a trick on Shirley and somehow switched places. The ground came up to meet her; her bubble gum popped out of her mouth. There was a quick stab of pain, and blood. She held the cry inside as she picked herself up and ran, blood gushing out of her right knee, to home plate and across the lot.

Nearing the steps of her building, she called out, "Ma, I'm hurt!" She looked at the gash in her knee. She knew it was deep. The blood was still pouring out. The sight of it made her feel weak and dizzy. She held on to the banister to steady herself.

Mrs. Cohen ran up from the basement. "What happened? Oh, my God." She ran back into the basement and came out with a towel, which she pressed against Shirley's knee while she helped her up the steps and into the apartment. Irv came up right behind them. "Hey, are you okay?"

"I have to stop the bleeding," said Mrs. Cohen,

helping Shirley to the couch in the dining room. "What happened out there?"

"I f-fell on a rock," said Shirley. She kept herself from crying. She had cried enough for one day. "I must've tripped on my laces."

"You've been hurt worse," said Irv. "Remember when you fell down the stairs and knocked your front teeth out? And how about the time you were building that scooter and hammered your thumb?"

"Irving, please," said Mrs. Cohen. "You're not helping."

The towel was wet and bloody. The only time Shirley had ever seen so much blood was when Morton fell and cut his wrist. She turned away from the sight of it.

"It looks like tomato juice," said Irv, trying to get Shirley to laugh.

When the blood stopped, Mrs. Cohen washed the wound with soap and water and cleaned it with hydrogen peroxide. Shirley winced. Then her mother held the wound closed for a few more minutes before wrapping a gauze bandage around it.

"Stay off your feet for a while," said her mother. "Lie down and rest." She closed the curtains, and Irv went outside while Shirley rested on the couch and listened to "The Romance of Helen Trent," the story of a woman "who sets out to prove . . . that romance can live in life at thirty-five and after."

The story, like so many other soap operas, had a tendency to put Shirley to sleep. She had always fought the sleep and won. She fought it this time, too.

Only this time she lost.

∘ *12* ∘

A tapping on the dining room window woke
her. She pulled the curtain aside and saw Morton,
Howie, Donnie, and Marilyn standing on the
porch, motioning for her to come out. Marilyn was
mouthing the words *chicken fat*.

Shirley got up from the couch. Her leg buckled
under her, and she fell back down. On her second
try, she made it to the kitchen.

"Where do you think you're going?" asked
Mrs. Cohen when she saw Shirley limping into
the kitchen and heading for the door.

"Out to collect fat."

"Not with that leg you aren't."

"I have to. The Victory Club needs me."

"They can get along without you for one day."

"But I have to, Ma. For Manny."

Her mother smiled softly and nodded. "All

right, go ahead. But don't overdo it. And wear this. Your resistance is low."

From a drawer in the pantry, Mrs. Cohen took out a small muslin bag attached to a string and tied it around Shirley's neck. The camphor bag. Every year, during the hottest part of the summer, polio season, Shirley wore one of these bags. All the kids wore one. The bags held small pieces of camphor. The smell of the camphor was supposed to keep away the polio germs.

With her camphor bag around her neck like a necklace, Shirley limped out onto the porch and described to the Victory Club the circumstances that led to her injury. They were very impressed.

"You'll probably get a scar," said Morton, who knew all about scars because he had so many of them.

"I bet it hurts real bad," said Marilyn.

"It's killing me," Shirley agreed.

Howie and Donnie suggested that Shirley wait for them while they did the collecting.

"You can help carry the fat when we're finished," said Donnie.

"I'm collecting, too," she insisted. "I'll take all the first floors, and the rest of you can do the second and third." If wounds didn't stop our boys overseas from fighting, they weren't going to stop Shirley either.

Shirley decided that Mrs. Kaluzna would be her first customer. She could always get fat from her mother later. She limped over to Mrs. Kaluzna's porch and knocked on the screen door.

"Oh, Shirley, darling," came a voice. "Come in."

Shirley opened the door and walked into the kitchen. Mrs. Kaluzna was lowering the flames under her steaming pots.

"I'll never make it on time," she said, pulling off her apron. She hustled over to the kitchen table and began removing the bobby pins from her pin curls. "I have a meeting to go to, and I'm late."

"The Consumptive Aid Society?" Shirley asked.

"No. Hadassah."

"I can come back later," said Shirley, turning to leave.

"No, no. I'm already late. So what does it matter if I'm late a few minutes more? Now, Shirley, darling, how can I help you?"

"Well, I was wondering if you had any extra fat. We're collecting."

"You need *schmaltz? Oy,* do I have *schmaltz.*"
She jiggled the flab on her arms and laughed.
"See, plenty of *schmaltz.*"

Still laughing at her own joke, Mrs. Kaluzna
walked over to the refrigerator, removed two jars
of chicken fat, and handed them to Shirley.

"Two jars? Gee, thanks, Mrs. Kaluzna."

"For you, anything. I'm sorry I don't have
any bags." And then, as if she had just noticed,
"Shirley, darling, what happened to your
knee?"

"Nothing much. Just a slight wound. Have a
good time at your meeting, Mrs. Kaluzna."

Shirley hobbled out the door and across the
porch. She tried making her way down the steps.
But each step sent a shot of pain up through her
leg. So she hopped down the rest of the steps on
her left foot.

She continued hobbling along the sidewalk to
the stairway at the other end of the building. She
was exhausted by the time she reached it. But she
was happy, too. She already had two jars of
chicken fat, and she had hardly begun.

Shirley hopped up to the first floor, where
there were three more apartments. They netted
her two more jars and a bag to carry them in.
When she was finished, she slid down the banister

to the sidewalk and sat down on the bottom step to rest and wait.

She could hear the other members of the Victory Club on the floors above her, and pretty soon they were running down the steps to join her.

Howie and Donnie were grinning.

"We collected eight jars," an excited Marilyn announced.

"Great," said Shirley. "I have four. So that makes twelve all together. All this fat should make plenty of ammunition."

"And that's just this building," said Morton. "Wait till we do the one across the lot."

Buoyed by their success, the members started across the lot, laughing and singing war songs. The songs gave Shirley strength and would send power to the boys overseas.

From the third floor Mrs. Lasky called down. "*Sha,* already. Too much noise. Always too much noise."

Shirley's mother, who was in the lot hanging laundry, called back up to her. "Mrs. Lasky, enjoy the noise. It won't last forever. One day they'll grow up and move away. Then, believe me, you'll miss the noise."

With her mother's words giving her even more strength, Shirley continued her march, barely noticing the stabs of pain that came with each step. She thought of the scar she'd probably get—that she hoped she'd get. It would be like a medal. Like a Purple Heart. Her badge of courage. Every time she looked at it, she'd remember how she had helped her country. She would think of Manny. Once again, President Roosevelt would be proud of her.

One evening the Victory Club gathered around the radio in Shirley's dining room. They were waiting for the president to make his acceptance speech after being nominated by the Democrats.

Shirley loved to hear the president speak. His voice was warm and friendly and reassuring. Whenever she heard him over the radio or saw him in the movies on *Movietone News,* she knew that everything would be all right, and America would win the war. He would keep America safe. He would never let Germany or Japan take over the world. She was sure that's how everyone on Thirteenth Street felt.

As soon as Roosevelt came on, Mrs. Cohen put away the velvet dress she was working on, Mr. Cohen folded up the newspaper he was reading, and Irv came running in from the porch.

Shirley listened to the speech and tried to

picture the president in his wheelchair. He had been stricken with polio when he was already a grown-up. She listened carefully, inspired by his words:

"What is the job before us in 1944? . . . To win the war—to win it fast, to win it overpoweringly."

The Victory Club cheered. Irv whistled.

"The people of the United States will decide this fall whether they wish to turn over this 1944 job . . . to inexperienced and immature hands . . ."

"No! Never!" the club shouted.

". . . or whether they wish to leave it to those who saw the danger from abroad . . . and carried the war to its present stages of success. . . . They will decide on the record—the record written on the seas, on the land, and in the skies."

The club members cheered again as they ran out onto the porch when the speech was over.

"We've got to do something to help Roosevelt," said Shirley. "We have to help win the war fast and overpoweringly."

"We already helped," said Marilyn. "We planted the garden. And we collected the chicken fat."

"Yeah," Morton agreed. "But now we have to find out what to do with the fat. It's not going to help anyone by sitting in the refrigerator."

The members had split up the eighteen jars of fat they collected and stored them in their refrigerators.

"All the posters I've seen so far have said HOUSEWIVES! SAVE WASTE FATS," Morton went on. "But they never say what to do with the stuff."

"I'm talking about something more important than gardens and fats," said Shirley. "We've got to do something about Otto. If he's really spying, he could be hurting the war effort."

In the quiet of the evening, they all sat on the steps to do some serious thinking. Most of the neighbors were still inside their apartments, listening to the radio. The Victory Club had the outside to themselves.

"I've got it!" Morton announced, jumping to his feet. "Otto is probably home, listening to his radio. Now's our chance to get into the garage."

"It's dark in there," said Marilyn.

"I've got a flashlight."

"And there are rats."

Shirley imagined the rats and shivered.

"It's now or never. Who wants to come and look with me?"

"I have to go home," said Marilyn. "It's late, and my mother's waiting."

"I'll be a lookout," said Howie.

"Me, too," said Donnie. "And if there's any trouble, I can always run home for help."

"I'll come with you, Morton," said Shirley, who immediately regretted the offer.

"Good. I'll go get my flashlight."

Shirley prayed for her mother to call her in. Or for Irv to come out and pester her. Where was he when she needed him? She didn't want to go into a rat-infested garage. And what if Otto caught them there?

"Here it is," said Morton, bounding down the steps and waving the flashlight. "Let's go."

Shirley hesitated. Then she slowly followed him to the garage. Howie and Donnie were behind her.

Shirley and Morton crept up to the garage door while Howie stood guard near the alley. Donnie stood watch in front of the garage so he could keep an eye on Otto's apartment.

"Let us know when the coast is clear," said Morton, fumbling with the flashlight.

Shirley stood trembling at the door. She didn't

know what she was more afraid of. The rats or Otto.

"It's all clear," Howie announced.

"All clear," Donnie repeated.

Shirley's heart was pounding in her ears. But it was more than pounding that she heard. There was a steady ticking sound coming from inside the garage. She put her head against the door.

"Morton, there's something ticking in here."

"Ticking?" He put his ear to the door. "You're right. Holy cow! There must be a bomb inside!"

Howie and Donnie came running. "A bomb? You're nuts!" said Howie.

"Listen for yourself."

Howie and Donnie put their heads against the door, too. "It sounds like a bomb to me," said Donnie.

"It couldn't be," said Shirley. "Why would Otto want to blow up this dumb garage?"

"He doesn't," Morton answered. "He's just making it here. To take somewhere else. Somewhere important."

"There's a naval base around here, remember?" said Howie. "Maybe that's his target."

"We'd better get in there," said Morton.

"I don't know about this," said Howie. "I think we should go get help."

"No time," said Morton. "Anyway, I know just what to do. I saw it in a movie once." He turned to Shirley. "Quick! Go in and get me a pail of water."

Shirley bolted up the steps to her kitchen. "There's a bomb in the garage!" she yelled, reaching for a pail under the sink and turning on the faucet. While the water ran into the pail, Shirley dashed into the dining room, where her family was still listening to the radio.

"You've got to come out. You won't believe what we found."

"It's getting late," said her mother. "Enough playing for one day."

"We're not playing. We heard ticking."

She ran back to the sink and turned off the water. The pail wasn't even half full, but she couldn't wait any longer. She lifted it out of the sink with both hands, and then, with the water sloshing in the pail, she moved as fast as she could, out the door and down the steps toward the garage.

"Hurry," Morton called to her. He ran to meet her and helped her carry the pail to the garage door.

"Where are the others?" Shirley asked.

"They couldn't wait. They ran for help. Now

the question is, how do we get inside? Maybe we should try to kick down the door."

"Did you try the knob?"

"Oh, right." Morton turned the knob, and the door opened easily to a darkened garage. Morton shined the flashlight at the spot the ticking seemed to be coming from. And then they saw it.

A mechanism of some kind was lying on a wooden orange crate. It was made up of all sorts of gears and wheels.

"That's it!" Morton shouted. "Let's bring the pail in."

Shirley held back. "Are you sure you know what to do? Because if you don't, you'll blow us both up."

"I told you. I saw it in a movie."

Shirley carried the pail into the garage and set it down near the doorway.

Without a word, Morton moved slowly toward the mechanism and stood in front of it. The ticking continued strong and steady. He handed the flashlight to Shirley.

"Shine the light on the bomb while I pick it up."

"Be careful," Shirley warned.

With trembling hands, Morton reached for the bomb. Shirley shielded her face with her hand.

But Morton stopped short. He couldn't bring himself to pick it up.

"Do it already," said Shirley.

He reached for it a second time, sweat trickling down his face. He carefully lifted the bomb and held it out in front of him. Shirley saw him in slow motion, moving toward the pail.

"Don't drop it," she prayed.

"I can't see!" Morton cried out. "Shine the light on the pail."

Still shielding her face, Shirley aimed the light on the pail as Morton carefully lowered the mechanism into the water. The ticking stopped.

Morton straightened up and wiped his forehead with the back of his hand. "Well, what do you know? It worked."

Shirley breathed a sigh of relief. "Okay, now, let's just get out of here." She hurried to the door.

"It's a good thing you saw that movie," she continued as they left the garage. "I can't wait to see Otto's face."

"Where's the bomb?" a voice interrupted.

Shirley and Morton turned around to see Howie running toward them. And behind Howie came Donnie, followed by his mother and father and the precinct captain and the sheriff of Cook County.

"We brought help," Donnie called.

Mr. and Mrs. Kaluzna came out to the back porch. "What happened?" Mrs. Kaluzna called. "Morton, did you find more cigarettes?"

From all sides, people came streaming into the lot. Shirley's mother and father and Irv came hurrying down the steps. So did Morton's mother and father and Harold.

"Hey, maybe they really did find a bomb," said Irv. "What luck."

"A bomb?" Mrs. Kaminsky shrieked. "Morton, you get away from there."

"Shirley, come over here," Mrs. Cohen called, with a wave of her hand.

By this time, the sheriff had reached the garage. "Okay, everybody, keep calm. Don't touch anything. Stay back."

To Shirley, the sheriff didn't look like a sheriff. He wasn't even wearing his uniform. He was dressed in shorts and a polo shirt and looked like an ordinary person. The precinct captain wore slacks and an undershirt.

"Okay, kids," said the sheriff, as he and the precinct captain pushed Shirley and Morton aside and went into the garage. "Let's see what you have here."

He took Morton's flashlight and shined it on the bomb sitting at the bottom of the pail.

"Interesting," said the precinct captain. "What do you suppose that is?"

"It's a bomb," Morton answered.

What kind of question was that? Shirley wondered. Of course it was a bomb. Anyone could see that. "It was ticking before," she informed him.

"Ticking, huh?" asked the sheriff. "Well, it sure isn't ticking anymore. You kids saw to that."

Shirley and Morton smiled at each other. Already they were being treated like heroes. They would probably get their pictures on the front page of the Chicago newspapers, with the headline: *Kids Save Naval Base from Destruction.* Maybe they would even be invited to Washington to meet President Roosevelt at the White House.

Shirley could just picture it. Because of their quick thinking and fast actions, she—Shirley Frances Cohen—and Morton Kaminsky would be seen by thousands of people on *Movietone News,* shaking hands with the president of the United States of America.

∘ *13* ∘

"My clock! Who did this to my clock?"

Otto was one of the last people to enter the garage. When Shirley first saw him approaching, she said to herself, Now he's in for it. Now everyone will see what he's been up to.

But here he was, standing over the pail and talking about a clock.

What clock?

Otto leaned over, stuck his hand in the pail, and lifted out the dripping bomb. "Who did this to my clock?"

"Your clock?" asked the sheriff. "This is yours?"

"Actually, it is Mrs. Lasky's clock. I was fixing it for her."

Shirley slipped behind her mother. Morton, Howie, and Donnie found their mothers, too.

"It does look more like a clock than a bomb," said the sheriff.

"A bomb?" Otto looked puzzled.

"Well, the kids here thought you . . . you know how kids are."

"I do not make bombs," said Otto. "I fix clocks. And radios. Almost anything." He flicked on the light in the garage.

Shirley hadn't even known there was a light in the garage. Someone should have told her. It would've made their search so much easier. On the other hand, there would have been no search. They would have immediately seen what Shirley saw now, when she peeked out from behind her mother's back.

Clocks and clock faces. Wheels and gears like those that made up their "bomb." Lamps and radios and toasters, all in various stages of repair.

Shirley could hear her neighbors muttering to each other. They sounded almost disappointed that the bomb was turning out to be nothing more than a clock. She and Morton had saved them all—from a clock!

Shirley felt everyone's eyes on her, and her face grew hot. She tore away from her mother and ran up the steps to the apartment.

In the darkened dining room, she sat on the

couch, feeling sorry for herself and thinking angry thoughts about Otto.

Otto, the sneak. He had probably replaced all the bombs with clocks once he knew the Victory Club was on to him. He had embarrassed her and the rest of the club in front of the whole neighborhood. Made fools of them. Probably at this very moment, everyone was laughing at them.

Shirley experienced an uncomfortable feeling inside. Maybe it was the salami and eggs she had had for supper. Or maybe it was the feeling that she really had known better. That deep down she had known the truth all along. Otto wasn't a spy. She had just wanted him to be one. And yet there were unanswered questions. Who had killed Stinky's kittens? And what about the shortwave radio?

"Bombs away!" Irv burst into Shirley's thoughts through the kitchen door and turned on the light in the dining room.

"Go away," said Shirley, squinting in the sudden brightness.

Irv dropped down on the couch next to her. "I can't believe it. You actually thought that that clock was a bomb?"

"Well, you would have, too, if you had heard it. It was ticking. And there weren't any numbers on it. How was I supposed to know it was a clock?"

Oh, no! Shirley slumped deeper into the couch. Mrs. Lasky's clock! The uncomfortable feeling inside grew stronger.

Shirley heard voices on the porch, followed by the opening and closing of the screen door. Her mother and father had come back in.

"The excitement is over," said her father, swinging the pail, now empty of both "bombs" and water. "Everyone's gone home. And poor Otto. I think he's still trying to figure out what happened. Did you see the expression on his face?"

Shirley had seen it. And she knew she'd never forget it. He had looked so bewildered, so hurt, standing there in front of all those people, with that dripping clock. She almost felt sorry for him. Imagine that. Feeling sorry for Otto.

Mrs. Cohen settled into a chair and let out a deep sigh, as if she were taking a great weight off her feet. Then she shook her head slowly, saying nothing more than "Shirley, Shirley." Which really meant, Shirley, Shirley, what am I going to do with you?

Shirley looked at her mother. "Shirley, Shirley, what?"

"I never thought you'd carry this spy nonsense so far. How could you do something like this to a nice man like Otto? Just imagine what could have happened if that spy story caught on and the whole neighborhood began to suspect him."

"I couldn't help it. He was acting very suspicious. And he's German. He sounded just like those Nazis in the war movies."

"So—because of his accent, and because he comes from Germany, you can't trust him? Don't you see how dangerous that idea is?"

Mr. Cohen went over to turn on the radio. "If you started to mistrust everyone who has an accent, half of this neighborhood would be in trouble."

"That's the problem with this world," said Mrs. Cohen, kicking off her shoes and leaning back against the chair. "People are too quick to make judgments. Too quick to find blame. They just make up their minds not to like someone. Without any real reason."

"Well, it's all over," said Shirley. "I'm going to stay as far away from Otto as I can."

Mrs. Cohen sat upright in her chair. "Think again. You've already stayed too far away. None of this would have ever happened if you had given yourself a chance to know him. Instead, you made him up. You owe Otto an apology."

Her mother was right. Shirley knew she owed him an apology. She just didn't want to hear that she did.

"And Mrs. Lasky, too," her father put in. "An apology and a new clock."

Shirley spent the rest of the evening in the dining room, watching the flies and bugs getting stuck on the flypaper hanging from the light fixture, thinking about the apologies to Otto and Mrs. Lasky, and wondering how many dimes she had in her dime bank.

° *14* °

Shirley slept restlessly that night. Maybe it was the heat. Or the mosquitoes. Or maybe it was the whole episode with Otto and the mixed-up feelings she had about him. There was the fear of facing him. And the disappointment in finding that he wasn't a spy. She had wanted so much to catch a spy.

The smell of pancakes woke her up. Still in her pajamas, she went into the kitchen and sat down at the table.

"Feeling better?" her mother asked, dropping spoonfuls of batter onto a frying pan.

Shirley shrugged and took a sip of the orange juice her mother had squeezed for her. Then she poured herself some milk and checked out the state on the Capitol Milk lid. Well, what do you know? she said to herself. North Dakota. The capital—Bismarck.

Her mother brought her a plate of pancakes and a carton of sour cream. Shirley topped the pancakes with the sour cream and ate them all. She was beginning to feel a little better—until Irv walked in and asked her, "Did you discover any more bombs today?"

Shirley didn't answer him, but Mrs. Cohen served him his pancakes, and as soon as he was finished, she chased him out of the house.

After he had gone, her mother sat down at the table. "Morton's mother and I spoke to Mrs. Lasky earlier, and everything has been taken care of. You'll have to speak to her yourself at some point, but that can wait for a while. Right now, the important thing is that you find Otto and apologize to him."

Shirley shook her head slightly. "I don't know if I can. I'm still afraid of him."

"Once you talk to him, you won't be afraid anymore," her mother said. "I'm sure of it."

Shirley got up from the table, and as she turned to leave, she looked back at her mother. "What about Morton? Shouldn't he have to apologize, too?"

"Morton will have to take care of Morton," said her mother. She gave Shirley a pat on the backside. "Go on now, and get dressed. And later you can get yourself a malted."

A malted. Well, maybe she would get one. Though she knew it would never again taste quite as good. She wondered who would be working the soda fountain now. Mr. Zelnick? How could she face him? She would have to talk about Manny. What would she say? But she knew she had to see him sooner or later. Anyway, she still had to pick up her pictures from him.

Shirley put on a shirt and a pair of jeans and walked over to get Morton. He owed Otto an apology, too. And it would be easier to apologize together.

The inside door to Morton's apartment was closed. Shirley opened the screen door and knocked. When there was no answer, she rang the bell. Still no answer. Where was he? She went over to the window and looked in. The kitchen was empty. Of all times for him to go away.

A small piece of chalk was lying on the window ledge. Shirley picked it up, then climbed over the rail down to the sidewalk. While she waited for Morton, she drew hopscotch squares on the sidewalk and went searching for something to toss with.

She picked up stones of different sizes and weights and tried pitching them into the numbered squares. Each one of them skipped back out again. She tried bottle caps and a Smith Brothers cough drop that she dug out of her pocket. Nothing worked.

"Try this," came a voice from behind. Startled, Shirley spun around. Otto was standing next to the steps, wearing his bib overalls and brown work shoes. He held something out to her. "Maybe this will work. It's flatter."

Shirley took the matchbook that he was offering her, then turned around and tossed it into the number-five square. It landed there and stayed put.

"It works," she said, staring at the sidewalk. She walked over to the matchbook and picked it up. Then she turned back to him. "Thank you."

Otto sat down on the steps, watching her, and Shirley was left standing there, not knowing what to say or how to say it. Could she just come right out and say, "Otto, I'm sorry I thought you were a spy"?

She glanced nervously around the lot for Morton. She was angry with him for not being there with her. It would serve him right if she blamed him for the destruction of the clock. Morton is the one who said there was a bomb in the garage, she thought to herself. He's the one who dumped the clock in the water. I just held the flashlight. But she couldn't do that. How could she blame Morton for something that was just as much her fault?

She didn't have to go along with him. But she had. Because she wanted to.

Stinky bounded into the lot and ran over to Shirley. Shirley was happy to see her. And happy for the short reprieve from Otto. Stinky rolled over on her back, and Shirley began scratching the cat's underside. Stinky's stomach felt empty now, without the kittens.

After getting all the attention she wanted from Shirley, Stinky ran over to visit Otto. He scratched her behind the ears. "The next time she has her babies in the basement, we have to be sure to keep the door closed. We have to keep other cats away."

"Other cats?" Shirley asked.

"It is possible that a cat came in and killed her kittens. The male cat, perhaps. I do not know for sure, but it happens."

"A cat would do that?"

Otto nodded. "I have heard that sometimes even a mother cat will kill her own babies."

"You mean Stinky? No, she would never do anything like that." Shirley looked at Stinky, who was lying on the step next to Otto with her eyes closed, enjoying his stroking.

"Not on purpose. But sometimes another cat can anger the mother. Agitate her. And in her confusion, she might even attack her own children."

"Well, Stinky didn't do that. I know it."

"I do, too," said Otto. "Probably it was a stray cat who came in and killed them."

"But why would cats behave that way?"

"It is in their nature. Animals cannot control what is in their nature. They act on instinct." Otto gave Stinky one final pat on the head before she ran off. He rested his elbow on the step above him. "Now with people, that is another matter. People have instincts, too, but they can make a choice in how they act. Right or wrong, they can choose."

Shirley thought about how she and Morton had made a choice. The trouble was, it was the wrong choice. They had made up their minds that Otto was a spy. She moved closer to Otto and took a deep breath. "Otto . . . um . . . about that clock. I'm sorry. We're sorry. We didn't know it was a clock. We thought—we thought . . ."

"Yes, I know. You thought it was a bomb."

Shirley lowered her eyes for a moment, then glanced back at him. "And we saw your radio."

"Ah, yes, the radio." He smiled. "With that radio I can hear the news coming all the way from across the ocean. I hear where the battles are and mark the places on my map. It helps pass the hours."

"We were wrong about you, I know, but we thought . . . well . . . you're German. We thought maybe you . . . were spying." She looked down at her shoes. Her laces were untied. Why did they always come untied?

"I am not surprised. This is not the first time."

Shirley looked up from her shoes. "The first time?"

"The first time I have been accused."

"Of being a spy?"

"I do not know of what. But everywhere I go, people hear me speak. They hear the German. They accuse with their eyes." He took a metal nut from his pocket and began fiddling with it.

"It has been like that ever since I ran from Germany. Almost five years now. It was not so bad in the beginning. But when the war started . . ." He shook his head.

Shirley moved slowly toward the stairway and leaned against the banister. "I don't understand. If you're German, why did you run away?"

"We had to. My wife and I. It was no longer safe for her to remain there. You see, she was Jewish."

Shirley felt her mouth drop. She had never

imagined Otto with a wife. Especially a Jewish wife. But where was she? Shirley was afraid to ask.

"We had to leave," Otto continued. "When Hitler came, he brought such madness. Such hatred for the Jews. It was the beginning of terrible times for them—and for the world. Jews were beaten and spit on—shamed in public. They lost their jobs. Germans were ordered not to buy from Jewish stores. Jewish children were removed from schools. And so much more . . ." He let out a deep sigh. "I cannot begin to tell you."

"Why didn't they just leave?" Shirley asked.

"Some did. But others thought things would get better. 'How much worse can it get?' they asked. 'We are good Germans. Didn't we fight for Germany in the last war? Our country will not turn on us.'

"My wife's father—he was one of those people who spoke that way. He, too, fought in the war. 'All this will die down,' he said.

"But things did not die down. They got worse. And then there was *Kristallnacht.*"

Shirley moved in closer and sat on the bottom step. *"Kristallnacht?"*

"The night of broken glass." He turned the metal nut around in his fingers as he spoke. "One night—almost six years ago—in November, the government sent people out to destroy all the stores owned by Jews. I myself was a manager in one of those stores—a small department store. Mobs smashed the windows of our store—and the other stores, too. They set fire to the synagogues. They attacked Jews in the streets—even in their homes—and arrested or killed them. All over Germany—Austria, too—fires burned. Broken glass everywhere. It was then that we knew we must leave—while we could. We were afraid of what might come."

Shirley shuddered and wrapped her arms around herself. If she and her family lived in Germany, would they have left right away? Or stayed until it was too late—and Hitler wouldn't let them out anymore?

"Did your wife's father leave with you?"

"No. He was one of those arrested. We never heard from him after that."

Shirley tried to imagine her mother and father—and Irv—being taken away, and never hearing from them again. She wrapped her arms even more tightly around herself.

They were both silent for a while. Finally Shirley asked, "What about your wife? What happened to her?"

"My Clara—she was killed. Last year . . . a car accident." The nut dropped out of his hand and landed next to his feet.

"Oh, Otto, I'm so sorry." She looked into his eyes and saw the hurt there.

Otto made no attempt to retrieve the nut. "Even if I had not had a Jewish wife, I would have left. I could not—I would not live in Hitler's Germany. I will never forget his shouting voice. Or his soldiers marching in their black boots."

"I don't understand. Why didn't the people there try to stop him?"

"Some did, but not many. Most Germans believe in what he is doing. And now his hatred has spread all over Europe."

Otto leaned over to pick up the nut, then stood up and walked down the stairs. He turned toward the garden. "You should thin those plants, you know. They will grow better. If you want, I can help you."

"We'd like that. Thank you."

He started to walk away but stopped to look back. "I like the songs you sing. You and your club. Keep singing. Sing for the war to end. For America to win."

Shirley watched Otto as he walked to the end

of the building and disappeared into his apartment. Slowly she climbed up the steps to her own apartment and to her mother, who seemed to be waiting for her. She wrapped her arms around her mother's waist.

"Oh, Ma," she said. "I saw it. I saw his share of trouble."

· *15* ·

Shirley stood in front of the hallway mirror and smiled at her reflection. The dress was just the way she liked a dress to be—if she had to like a dress at all. No puffs, no frills. Just plain and simple. The blue velvet reflected the blue in her eyes.

She didn't remain in the dress for long. It was too hot in the apartment. So she slipped into a shirt and a pair of shorts and went out to get her pictures from Zelnick's. She was ready for them.

The sky above Independence was blue and cloudless. And up ahead Shirley could see a sailor walking toward her. She wondered if he would soon be going off to war. When he came closer, she looked up at him and said a silent prayer. Come home safely, sailor.

She continued on and rounded the curve to Douglas Boulevard. When she reached Zelnick's, Shirley came to an abrupt halt. Her heart felt like it was going to drop down to her feet. There, in the window of the drugstore, was the small white flag with the gold star. Manny's gold star. She stood in the middle of the sidewalk, staring at it. The star was supposed to have been blue. Why wasn't it blue?

Through the open door she could see Mr. Zelnick inside, waiting on a customer. She paused a moment, then walked in. She glanced at the soda fountain, half expecting to see Manny there. Instead, she saw an old man serving ice cream to some small children. She turned away.

"I was wondering when you were going to come. It's been a while."

"What?" Shirley looked in the direction of the prescription counter.

Mr. Zelnick was standing there, holding out a large envelope. "Your pictures. I was wondering when you were going to pick them up."

Slowly Shirley approached the counter, managed a weak smile, and took the envelope. She paid him and began looking through the pictures. There was the picture of the club's first meeting, with Stinky on her lap and everyone saying *cheese*. And the one her mother took of the club sitting on the steps, wearing their Roosevelt badges, and there were Morton's cigarettes, and— Shirley froze.

"What's wrong? Didn't they come out good?"

Shirley looked up at Mr. Zelnick with blurry eyes.

"Why, Shirley, what's the matter?"

She handed him the picture. With a questioning look, he took it from her. His eyes held the photograph for a long time. Through her own tears, Shirley saw his.

"It troubled me," said Mr. Zelnick, "that I didn't have a recent picture of him. But Manny told me not to worry. He said he would send me one of him in his uniform. Only he never got the chance." He wiped his eyes.

But he *was* in uniform, Shirley thought—his white apron. That was the way she had usually seen him. And that was the way she would remember him.

"This must be the last picture ever taken of him," Mr. Zelnick said.

"You can have it."

He nodded. "I can't tell you . . . well, it means a lot."

"I know," she said. "I miss him, too. It's not the same without him."

"No, it's not," said Mr. Zelnick. "And we had such plans. Manny was going to become a druggist and work with me here in the pharmacy."

The pharmacy? She looked around the prescription counter where Mr. Zelnick spent so much time. "Well, what do you know?" she whispered. "So this is a pharmacy."

"It's what he always wanted to do, ever since he was small," said Mr. Zelnick.

"He would have been good at it," said Shirley, smiling at him and placing the rest of the pictures back in the envelope. She turned and headed toward the door. She would return later to have a copy of Manny's picture made for herself. With the smile still on her face, Shirley walked out of Zelnick's Drugstore.

The heat hung over Thirteenth Street all day. After supper, Shirley's mother sliced some watermelon and packed it up, along with some blankets, to take to the park, where they would spend the rest of the evening trying to cool off.

Shirley gathered her pictures to show to Morton and the rest of the club. Well, they weren't a club anymore. Not since all that trouble began.

176

Shirley also had with her the shuffleboard set, which had finally arrived in the afternoon mail. She had been so excited when it came. But it wasn't at all what she had expected.

"A crummy window shade?" she had cried out after she unrolled the shuffleboard on the hallway floor in her apartment. "This is what they sent me after all this time?" It was yellow and coated with wax, just like the window shade in her kitchen. The only difference was, there were black, numbered squares printed on the shuffle-board. The set also came with some cheap-looking cues and disks. In spite of her disappointment, she decided to take it to the park in case someone got bored and wanted to play with it.

Shirley and her family walked across the lot toward the park. Her father carried one card-table chair, and Irv carried another. "It's going to be a hot one tonight," said Mr. Cohen as they crossed Independence Boulevard.

"Let's sleep there all night and not come home until tomorrow," Shirley suggested.

"If we sleep there until midnight, it'll be to-morrow," said Irv, finishing a banana Popsicle and dropping the stick down Shirley's back.

"Hey, cut it out!"

"Irving, behave yourself," Mrs. Cohen warned.

Morton and Marilyn were already in the park with their families. So were Mr. and Mrs. Kaluzna. The whole block seemed to be there. Even the precinct captain and the sheriff of Cook County.

Shirley spread out the blankets just as Morton and Marilyn ran over to her. "Why did you bring a window shade to the park?" Marilyn asked.

"That's my shuffleboard. Maybe we can play later. But first, do you want to see the pictures I took?"

"Great!" said Morton.

"Oh, I love to look at pictures," said Marilyn, dropping onto the blanket.

Shirley handed her the pictures one at a time, and Marilyn passed them to Morton. "Try not to get your fingerprints on them," Shirley cautioned.

Pretty soon Howie and Donnie came by. "Oh, good, pictures," said Donnie, and he and Howie joined the others on the blanket.

They passed around the pictures of themselves at their meetings. There they were, grinning into the camera and wearing their armbands. They laughed at Stinky following Morton and Shirley on the fence and at the cartons of Lucky Strikes. They admired the carrot and radish plants in their victory garden and groaned at the sight of their failed watermelon plants. There was even a picture of the bottom half of Irv's face.

"Hey, look at that handsome guy," said Irv, peeking over their shoulders. Shirley ignored him.

Together they looked over the pictures of their summer. Their summer memories. It had been an exciting summer so far, even if they hadn't ended any wars. They had almost started one, though. Maybe, thought Shirley, it was easier to start wars than it was to end them.

Irv spotted Ivan and ran off. Then Marilyn got up from the blanket and started running. "Who wants to play tag?"

Howie and Donnie chased after her, and Shirley and Morton remained on the blanket, still looking through the pictures. In the background she could hear the adults talking among themselves. The old people spoke with Yiddish accents, and Shirley wondered then, as she often did, whether she would suddenly begin speaking with a Yiddish accent when she grew into an old lady. She decided not to worry about that now. It would be a long time before she got old.

She noticed Mrs. Kaminsky watching them, and she knew just what was in her thoughts. She could almost hear the half sentences. "There's nothing I'd like better than for you and Morton . . . who knows, maybe someday . . ."

Well, she wasn't going to marry Morton. She liked him as a friend, but she could never picture herself being married to him. She imagined being married to someone tall, dark, and handsome, like Tyrone Power or Robert Taylor. Or to someone cute, like Gene Kelly. They could dance off into the sunset.

Now the sun was setting behind the Sefard Synagogue, where Shirley and her family would spend the High Holidays, and where she would wear her blue velvet dress and pray for the war to end.

Somewhere during her thoughts, Morton had left, and Shirley remained on the blanket alone, listening to the adult voices floating on the warm summer breezes. Voices that spoke of war and Hitler and worry over families who hadn't been heard from since Hitler and the black boots began marching across Europe. Shirley would pray for all the families, too. She would pray for President Roosevelt to do something to help the Jews.

As dusk turned to night, fireflies flickered in the darkness. Shirley stretched out on the blanket and gazed at the star-gilded sky. So many stars. There had to be one for each of our boys overseas.

One star, an especially bright star, winked at her. And Shirley knew it was Manny's star. She winked back.

A soft breeze washed over her, and for now all was quiet on the home front.